M000074547

SEAL IN A STORM

SILVER SEALS SERIES BOOK 5, CONNECTED TO GUARDIAN ELITE SERIES

KALYN COOPER

SEAL in a Storm

E-Book Published by KaLyn Cooper, Black Swan Publishing 2019
Print version Published by KaLyn Cooper, Black Swan Publishing 2019
ISBN-13: 978-1-970145-09-0

Copyright © 2019, KaLyn Cooper

All rights reserved. Except as permitted under the U.S. Copyright Act of
1976, no part of this publication may be reproduced, distributed, or
transmitted in any form or by any means, or stored in a database or
retrieval system, without the prior written permission of the author.

This book is a work of fiction.

Names of characters, places, and events are the construction of the author,
except those locations that are well-known and of general knowledge, and
all are used fictitiously. Any resemblance to persons living or dead is
coincidental, and great care was taken to design places, locations, or
businesses that fit into the regional landscape without actual
identification; as such, resemblance to actual places, locations, or
businesses is coincidental. Any mention of a branded item, artistic work,
or well-known business establishment, is used for authenticity in the work
of fiction and was chosen by the author because of personal preference, its
high quality, or the authenticity it lends to the work of fiction; the author
has received no remuneration, either monetary or in-kind, for use of said
product names, artistic work, or business establishments, and mention is
not intended as advertising, nor does it constitute an endorsement. The
author is solely responsible for content.

Cover Artist: Becky McGraw
Editors: Trenda London and Rebecca Hodgkins
Formatting by: Drue Hoffman, Buoni Amici Press.

I dedicate this book to my father who passed away while I was writing it. As children, we were enthralled by his stories that interwove a limited amount of tangible truth with outlandish lies. Thank you, Daddy, for giving me this late-in-life career. You will be missed!

ACKNOWLEDGMENTS

I would like to thank my Suspense Sisters for including me in this new wave of Silver SEALs. SEAL in a Storm was fun to write with its mature characters and their seasoned romance.

A big thank you goes to the Ladies of Black Swan Book Club. This Facebook group helps me in so many ways with every book.

My unending thanks goes to my editors who worked long hours, practically editing as I wrote, to meet my deadlines after my father passed away. Trenda London, my content editor, helped me think through many scenes, getting the correct point of view. May God bless the heart of my copy editor, Rebecca Hodgkins, who corrected Dragon-isms and my lack of commas.

Once again, a special thanks goes to my wonderful friend and military romantic suspense author, Caitlin O'Leary. Her twisted plotting made this book more interesting.

As always, I thank Drue Hoffman, the best publicist I could have, because she puts up with me.

I can't thank my husband enough for being there for me, whether he's holding me at my father's funeral, or cooking supper because I'm on deadline.

I couldn't do this without my tribe. I truly appreciate each and every one of you.

ABOUT THIS BOOK

There is a storm brewing...in his heart...Her name is Rayne.

As a former SEAL commander, Dex Carson had participated in more than his share of rescues. When called upon to lead a multi-agency team into the Virgin Islands National Park jungle to rescue high value targets, he knew he was headed for trouble. Ten teenage girls—whose parents were members of Congress—and their chaperones, needed saving from kidnappers. He cringed. The thought of entitled children and diva mothers made him clench his teeth. When he saw *she* was on his team, he was ready to quit. His heart couldn't take it. But a SEAL never quits.

At forty-two, Rayne Yoshida felt too old to go tromping through the jungle after the Speaker of the House's new wife and daughter. The recalcitrant prima donna had had rejected the advice of her husband's Secret Service protection and followed her sweet-as-sugar stepdaughter to the Caribbean on a student work/adventure trip. But as Agent in Charge of the

Speaker's detail, Rayne had to go. Her mood darkened when she saw their team leader, the bull-headed, bossy, but oh so sexy, Dex Carson. They had history...that had almost gotten her fired.

With a hurricane bearing down on the tiny island, they only have days to find and rescue the girls and their chaperones...and keep their hands off each other.

This sizzling military romance features a seasoned hero and heroine, second chances, and edge of your seat suspense. SEAL in a Storm is part of the Suspense Sisters new wave of connected books, Silver SEALs.

LETTER TO READERS

Thank you so much for purchasing *SEAL in a Storm*!

I was so excited to be asked to join the Suspense Sisters in their second wave, Silver SEALs. Please be sure to read all twelve full-length novels after reading the Prequel. These stories are all military romantic suspense with seasoned (mature) characters. A complete list is available at the end of this book as well as a sneak peek at Kris Michaels' SEAL Forever.

SEAL in a Storm features Dex Carson, first introduced in *Securing Willow*. Although not numbered or identified as such, *SEAL in a Storm* is to be considered book number six in the **Guardian Elite** series which is a spinoff from the **Black Swan** series.

Every book I write is a standalone, but for deeper understanding of the characters you might consider reading the following:

CHAPTER ONE

Dex Carson eased the throttle forward, taking his pride and joy slowly away from the dock. He glanced back at his pickup and boat trailer sitting in the parking lot with a dozen others.

It will be fine. Deep down he knew it was secure, but after twenty-two years active duty, most of them as a Navy SEAL, he had very little trust and confidence in his fellow man. Or woman, for that matter.

As soon as he cleared the marina, he shoved the stick forward, giving *Reel Peace*, his nearly new bass boat, lots of gas. The bow came up on plane and Dex adjusted the trim, so it rode smoothly over Smith Mountain Lake. The wind in his face was clean and crisp, so different from the naval ships he had been on so many times throughout his career. No matter where you went on an aircraft carrier, it smelled like hot asphalt or burning tires. On the destroyers and cruisers, he couldn't take a deep breath without inhaling diesel fumes. Unless the submarine had recently surfaced, the recycled air smelled of cooking food, sweaty men, and stinky socks.

Personally, Dex had always preferred riding in the Zodiacs. He might be old-school, but those little boats could flat out run, and had saved his life more than once.

Nudging the stick forward another inch, he grinned as the powerful outboard motor growled, pushing his nineteen-foot bass boat faster through the sparkling fresh water.

As he zipped down the lake, he watched the muddy purple sky turn lilac before strands of pink pushed away the darkness to allow the golden rays of the sun to announce the day.

Shifting the map to orient himself, Dex hoped the extended conversation he had with the salty old Navy chief at the bait store would prove promising. Catching a couple three- or four-pound largemouth bass to freeze and take home with him would be wonderful, but fighting a forty-inch striped bass would definitely make his day. Hell, maybe his month. Who was he kidding? It could be a lifetime event.

He glanced down at the map before turning into a cove and pulled up on the throttle, idling the boat. He was sure this was the place the retired Senior Chief Petty Officer had indicated.

Dex flipped on his electronic fishfinder. Holy fuck, there were a lot of fish down there. His anticipation grew. After covering the cove in a grid pattern, he picked a spot and turned off the engine. Dropping the trolling motor over the gunwale, he tamped down his excitement. Everything felt right. The chill of the October morning, the quiet cove on the peaceful lake, the curve of the sun peeking above the mountains to the east, nothing but him and the fish in the water below his beautiful boat. This was how Dex had always envisioned his retirement.

Within minutes he was casting.

He sat down in the raised seat in the bow and let out a deep breath.

This was his little slice of heaven. His reward for serving his country. He could now do exactly what he wanted, when he wanted. There was no one who outranked him, ordering him on one more mission. Or worse, forcing him to order good young men to put their lives at risk. And damn it, they were *all* good, and too fucking young.

That was the great thing about working for Guardian Security. He got to pick and choose his assignments. The decision was his, and his alone. The Guardian Elite men who went on those missions were all volunteers and well-seasoned operators. They too had the choice of go or no go.

Dex had loved coordinating the support for the mission in Venezuela last month. Alex Wolf, the owner of the company, had allowed him flexible hours out of the Miami Center rather than his usual office in DC. Every night, Dex would talk to Remi Steel as they figured out what was needed and by noon the next day, Dex would have it on its way to Caracas.

Then, he would take the afternoon off and spend a couple hours enjoying the company perks, such as their own personal indoor shooting range, a world-class gym, sparring arena, or chilling in the apartment assigned to him. Sometimes he'd just go to the beach and swim for hours in the warm Gulf Stream.

Several of the younger men, all former special operators, invited him to join them at the nightclubs. Loud pounding music, scantily clad girls young enough to be his daughters, and watered-down drinks, wasn't Dex's idea of a good time. Twenty years ago, he would've been right there with them, but at forty-four years old, he wasn't looking for a quick fuck with some little girl with a daddy complex.

He wasn't looking for a woman in any way, shape, or form. He'd been married, twice, and was not about to test the theory that third time was a charm.

Dex peered at the fishfinder, then cast toward the large fish meandering close to the shore.

He stared at the water and started to calculate the ages of Jan's kids. They had to be ten and twelve years old. No. They were older than that.

He married her right out of college and dragged her to Officer Candidate School in Newport, Rhode Island. She was not happy to get packed up twelve weeks later and moved to San Diego for SEAL training where he was seldom home. Even though she had a bachelor's degree in economics, it was impossible to find a job using her education. To make matters worse, there were very few officers in BUD/S and only a couple were married. She was alone much of the time and unhappy all the time. Dex didn't need that kind of stress at home. He had plenty in SEAL training. They were divorced before he ever pinned on his Trident.

She moved back home to the small town in Indiana where her parents, brothers and sister, a dozen aunts and uncles, and three sets of grandparents still lived. Before he'd left on his first overseas deployment, she was already married to an accountant and pregnant.

Some women just aren't cut out to be military wives.

He felt a little tug on the line. "Come on, baby. You want that little bug. I know you do." He purposely kept his voice low.

The next tug was a little harder.

He yanked the pole upright to set the hook and started reeling in. The fish tried to swim away but he was no match for Dex. As he pulled it up beside the boat, he grabbed the net and scooped the largemouth bass out of the water. He reached into the side pocket of his cargo shorts for his multi tool and extracted the hook from the fish's mouth.

Damn. Nice size. Its fillets would make a great supper. He slid the fish into the live tank. A few more like that and he'd be set for weeks.

Dex immediately baited his hook again and checked the fishfinder. He cast almost to the same spot then sat back down in the chair.

His mind wandered to his second wife, a gorgeous brunette he'd met at one of the many team parties on Virginia Beach. A fellow Lieutenant JG's wife had introduced him to her college roommate, Genevieve. They'd sat on beach chairs and dug their toes into the soft sand, talking for hours about everything from baseball to international politics while drinking beer and cooling-off with dips in the ocean.

She was an electrical engineer for the local government contractor. She was perfect. Intelligent, self-sufficient, excellent social skills, and she didn't get upset if he was called away suddenly and out of contact for weeks. After about six months of what Dex considered normal dating, he asked her to move into his apartment. Hell, he was only there half the time anyway. They were married before they'd known each other a full year.

The tip of his pole moved an eighth of an inch. He slowly pulled back on it a little to tease the fish, enticing it to take a big bite. He felt the moment the fish latched on and he yanked hard to set the hook.

Damn. He was going to have to be sure to thank the old sailor. The man certainly knew the lake. The fish had his pole bowed over but was still about twenty feet away, when Dex's phone rang.

Fuck. He certainly wasn't going to let this fish go just to answer a telemarketer's call. As he pulled and cranked the reel, the phone quit ringing.

Dex had his prey next to the boat when the ringing started again.

Persistent fuckers. Ignoring his phone, he concentrated on pulling the fish into the boat.

Hot damn. Another largemouth. This one was even bigger than the last. After removing the hook, he tossed the fish into the live well.

It was going to be a good day.

Then his phone rang again.

Dex reached into the brown paper bag for another bug.

Maybe the call was from Alex, checking to see that everything was okay at his fiancée's family's house. Or maybe he was calling to let Dex know that he might be getting company. The beautiful home could sleep more than a dozen. He'd been told it was often rented out for family reunions and corporate retreats. With over a hundred feet of waterfront, a large boathouse and dock, not to mention the deck that was twice the size of his apartment, Dex had rambled the huge empty house last night before settling down.

The phone rang incessantly.

He flicked the bug into the water, watched it struggle for a second before the biggest bass Dex had ever seen rose from the water, mouth open. It grabbed the flailing insect before diving back in. Dex grinned at the sight. That sight was better than a pod of whales breaching.

With a sigh, he extracted his phone from a side cargo pocket. Squinting at the caller ID, Dex wondered what *he* wanted.

"Please tell me you called for a fucking good reason because, honest to God, the big one just got away."

"No time for small talk, old friend." Former Lieutenant Commander Silas Branson sounded serious. "Yours isn't a secure line so I can't talk—"

Why the hell would Si need a secure line? Dex figured he'd find out in just a moment. "Give me thirty seconds and it can be." Another advantage of working for Guardian Security. Alex wanted to be able to get in touch with his men on a secure line anytime, anywhere. After pressing a sequence of numbers, a green light came on the screen. "Okay, Crash, we're now completely secure. What's up?"

"You probably know that I now work for the Department of Homeland Security."

"I heard something about that," Dex confirmed. "I also heard you worked your way pretty far up that ladder."

"High enough that they've allowed me to create a special division, emphasis on the word *special*." Crash was obviously fishing for recruits. Maybe he was building something like the CIA's Special Operations Group. Those were one hundred of the deadliest men in the world.

No. Dex was too old for that shit. SOG was boots on the ground. At this point in his life, he thoroughly enjoyed sleeping in a soft bed every night, eating delicious hot food prepared by somebody else, while coordinating a mission thousands of miles away. Those are jobs for younger men.

He was already part of an awesome team of special operators. He had a really good thing going with Alex. He wasn't interested in joining anything controlled by the government, least of all for Homeland Security. If those guys got their claws into him, they'd have him by the balls, and he'd be right back taking orders, or giving them.

"Look, Si, I'm really honored that you'd consider me to be on your new te—"

"I know about Venezuela. You'd be the team leader. In complete control. One mission only." Si was dangling that bait in front of him.

Dex looked at his newfound fishing hole and wondered how soon they would need him.

"What's the mission?" There were some things that Dex had done, because his country had asked him to, that he just wouldn't do these days.

"Kidnapping."

Silas was really tempting him. Dex had been involved in dozens of rescues, and although each one was unique, every mission he'd been on was successful.

"Why aren't they sending in a SEAL Team?" He hadn't been gone *that* long, had he? Could they have moved international kidnapping missions away from SpecOps?

Silas sighed. "They can't. They were taken on U.S. soil."

"That sounds like a job for the FBI. Aren't those guys the experts, at least at home?" Dex reconsidered for a second. "Or are they outside CONUS?" he asked, referring to the continental USA.

"Yes. They were captured in the U.S. Virgin Islands."

"They?" Damn. There was more than one. That exponentially complicated the entire situation.

"*They* must be damn important," Dex noted.

There was a long pause before Silas answered. "Approximately three hours ago, ten teenage girls, their teacher, and three female chaperones were taken on St. John Island in the Caribbean."

"Fuck." Dex lowered his body into the bow fishing chair while holding the phone to his ear.

"These aren't just any little girls," Silas explained. "Their parents are all congressmen and senators... including the daughter of the Speaker of the House."

As he digested all the information, Silas kept talking, dangling that bait closer and closer to Dex. "I know this is a lot to take in all at once, but the clock is ticking. You're the right man for this job."

"Why me?" Dex wondered aloud.

"They were taken by the Boko Haram." Silas had just set the hook.

He'd dealt with the terrorist organization twice in his career. Five years ago, when they had kidnapped over two hundred and fifty little girls from schools in Nigeria to become unwilling brides to their soldiers. His SEAL teams had helped free dozens of them during the following months. The extremists had freed a few more over the next several years, and some had escaped. All who had made it to freedom had been badly mistreated, and they told horror stories of rape, starvation, and beatings.

Dex would be thrilled to bring some of the jihadist terrorists to justice...or simply rid the world of their existence.

The man he really wanted in his crosshairs was its leader, Aahil Mohammed Jaja. Twelve years ago, that fucker had masterminded the theft of nearly two million credit card numbers from U.S. citizens and escaped with over four million dollars. No one was sure if he was the computer guru or if someone worked for him. It was a verified fact, though, that Jaja had a genius IQ and a photographic memory.

Working alongside U.S. Secret Service special agents, the young Lieutenant Dex Carson's SEAL team had gone after Jaja. Although they were able to capture several of Jaja's highest-ranking men, they had missed the terrorist leader by minutes.

Thoughts of that mission automatically brought along memories of Rayne Yoshida. His night with her ranked in the top five best ever.

The disastrous morning after was definitely the worst day of his life. If he ever saw that little bitch again, he might just kill her. Or maybe he'd strip her naked for a repeat, first.

"Dex, every second counts with these hostages. I need your decision." Si's bait was far too tempting.

"I'm in." Hook. Line. And sinker. "This one mission, only, I want that to be clear," Dex confirmed. He heard the all-too-familiar distant *whomp, whomp* of helicopters and automatically looked to the east. Silhouetted by the rising sun was a pair of Black Hawks headed his way.

Dex chuckled. "You knew I was going to say yes, didn't you?"

"They'll meet you at your truck. You'd better get that bass boat pointed down the lake. I'll see you when you get here. Branson out." The line went dead.

Leaping out of his chair, he quickly pulled up the

trolling motor and started the big engines. He slammed the throttle all the way forward, pushing the engine as hard as he dared.

Every second counted. Lives were at stake.

He had the biggest fish of his life to catch.

CHAPTER TWO

"Deputy Director O'Brien, I feel that I would be an asset to the joint task force and the rescue team." Rayne Yoshida was prepared to list, and explain in detail, all the reasons why she was qualified for this mission.

The nearly bald man glanced up from his desk. "I'm sure the Speaker's daughter and wife would prefer to see your friendly female face rather than some big behemoth with face paint wearing camouflage and guns."

"I'm sure she would, sir." Rayne didn't want to point out the fact that she, too, would be wearing camouflage and grease paint and carrying several weapons. This was a covert mission and not her first.

"Have you increased personal protection on the Speaker of the House?" DD O'Brien watched her for any quirk or twitch. Everyone at the Secret Service was trained to be ultra-cognizant of body language. "Aahil Mohammed Jaja may have taken little Callie and Angelique on purpose. They may have been his primary target, and the others nothing more than collateral for him."

"But he put Linda Thompson as spokesperson on the video," she protested. "Her husband is the Chairman of the Senate Armed Forces Committee. Jaja is very smart." The man in question spoke four languages, including English, and although he'd studied religion at the university level, he purportedly had been quite the computer hacker.

Rayne had never been convinced that it was Jaja who had hacked into one of the largest banking companies in the United States and stolen millions of credit card numbers. There was definitely a chain, though, linking the millions of stolen dollars to the financing of his Islamic radical group, Boko Haram. She had hoped, though, that she had captured the real culprit when she ran the Northern Africa Secret Service Office. The fact that there had never been another Internet theft as big as the one twelve years ago was proof enough to her that the real hacker was serving time somewhere..

Her boss leaned back in his chair. Resting his elbows on the arms, he steepled his fingers. "Did you find it odd that he didn't ask for anything? And if he's as smart as you believe, is this a diversionary tactic for something bigger?"

"To answer your first question, yes, I have doubled the personal protection for Congressman Sedgwick. We have varied his routine even more drastically and his chief of staff has cleared his appointment calendar. There are three pieces of legislation coming before Congress in the next few days that he'll be required to oversee the vote." As senior special agent in charge of personal security for Robert Sedgwick, the Speaker of the House, Rayne had personally chosen his detail. Technically, he was third in line to the White House, thus one of the most important men in U.S. politics.

Earning the agency's trust and confidence after the Nigeria debacle had taken her years and a change in career path from the Office of Strategic Intelligence and Information to the Office of Protected Operations. She was currently the highest-ranking woman in her division.

"Addressing your first point about Callie and Angelique Sedgwick's capture, until Jaja makes his demands, I'm not sure if he knows exactly who he has kidnapped other than fourteen politically connected females." Rayne had studied the man for years after he'd slipped through her fingers over a decade ago.

Without letting her boss speak, she continued, "In answer to your second question, no, I didn't necessarily find it unusual that Jaja has not yet stated his demands. When he kidnapped all those young girls five years ago, he never asked anyone for anything because he never intended to use them as hostages. Those were brides to appease his soldiers to improve his power over his followers. His second round of female kidnappings, approximately a year later, was a completely different situation. When he took both young girls and adult women, he was willing to trade the latter in exchange for freeing some of his senior-level soldiers, keeping the virgins, once again, for his men."

Her middle-aged boss, and father of five, shook his head. "That just makes me sick. You know I have daughters in that same age group. I'd want to ki—,"

"Don't go there, sir," Rayne interrupted. "I'm not convinced that Jaja is going to try to move ten little girls across the Atlantic Ocean and all the way to Nigeria just to provide infidel virgins to his soldiers. He's going to have a hard-enough time trying to escape with the men he's obviously brought with him."

"Now, to your final question, do I believe this is a diversionary tactic?" She had to keep him focused on the situation. The task force was meeting over at the Department of Homeland Security in just over an hour and she wanted to be there. She needed to be on that team. "No. Everyone in this building knows that terrorists walk among us and are a viable threat to our way of life and to the leaders of our country. I truly believe that Jaja wants something that only our highest-ranking leadership can provide. What that is," she shrugged. "I don't know. Personally, I'm just glad he is so self-centered that he sent a video to the President. Last time he wanted to speak to someone in power, he put it on YouTube. At least this way, we can keep the press out of it and the general public from armchair coaching."

The deputy director furrowed his brow. "That doesn't mean that he won't release it on the Internet, or send it directly to the Washington Post, if he doesn't like how the situation is handled."

"Speaking of handling the situation," Rayne tried to redirect the conversation once again, "Sir, would you put me on the task force rescue team as the Secret Service representative?"

The clock was ticking. He stared at her as though considering her request. Dressed in what she thought of as her uniform of black slacks, white crisp cotton button-down blouse, custom-cut black jacket that concealed her shoulder holster, reflective sunglasses hooked on the edge of her jacket pocket, she looked ready for the streets of DC, but not the jungle on St. John Island.

Reaching for the phone, he looked at her. "I'm calling the director of operations at Homeland Security. You had better get moving. I'll text you the meeting room."

"Thank you, sir." Rayne spun on her heel and headed toward the door.

"Special Agent Yoshida," he called as she reached for the knob. "Don't fuck this up, and I mean that literally. I don't want a repeat of Nigeria on my watch."

She felt the verbal slap all the way to her professionally-hardened heart as it dropped to her stomach and made her queasy. After years of exemplary performance, complete dedication to her job on the clock and off, it took only one sentence to put her right back to where she was twelve years ago...in trouble and fighting to keep her position.

"Deputy Director O'Brien, I can assure you that will never happen again." Rayne had learned her lesson the first time she let her guard down and allowed a sexy SEAL to help her burn off the aftermath of an adrenaline rush. Besides, no one had ever piqued her interest the way Dex Carson had before, during, and after that mission.

After rushing to the assigned room at the Department of Homeland Security, Rayne set her large duffel at the end of the row of bags. She slid into an empty chair at the conference table and glanced around.

"Ladies. Gentlemen. Welcome. I'm Silas Branson, the chairman of this multi-agency task force. Each of you has been selected for your unique skill set and knowledge. The clock is ticking on these kidnapped women and children, so let's get started so we can get the team on its way." The large man with broad shoulders and military demeanor ordered the lights to be dimmed.

The man to her left slid Rayne the briefing jacket as others were distributed.

"Sometime last night, ten girls and their three female chaperones were taken from their tents at Cinnamon Bay on St. John Island." A picture of large green tents sitting atop wooden platforms with waterproof tarps draped over top appeared on the screen, immediately followed by an inside view of four cots, suitcases, and bright-colored clothes strewn everywhere. A slash running vertically on the backside facing the jungle dominated the next shot.

Rayne controlled her breathing as she sucked in air when she really wanted to gasp. She could only imagine how scared Callie had been as someone cut through her tent and grabbed her, pulling her through that slit and into the jungle.

"These pictures were uploaded to us nearly an hour ago by the Park Rangers who were sent to the campground to confirm that they were no longer there." photographs of boot prints in the sand, and what Rayne would consider crime scene photos, continued to flash on the screen, a light pierced the room as someone entered. The newcomer strode directly to Mr. Branson, whispered in his ear, then took the seat right next to him.

Rayne couldn't make out his face in the dark room, but there was something familiar about the new man. Maybe it was the way he walked? He was square shouldered, his footsteps nearly silent. Her danger radar didn't blip so she shook it off.

A map of the Caribbean appeared on the large flat screen behind the chairman. Rayne thought it was interesting that Branson never called himself by any official title. In the competitive pool of civil service, she couldn't believe he hadn't thrown out his designation.

Opening the book in front of her, she squinted to see how he was listed.

Damn it. She couldn't see a thing.

The picture on the flat screen zoomed in on the U.S.

Virgin Islands, then specifically on St. John Island. Green covered nearly the entire land designating it as Virgin Islands National Park.

"There are nearly thirteen thousand acres of protected land. As you can see, a road unevenly bisects the island." Using a laser pointer, Branson traced several lines off to each side. "These are several of the hiking trails through the jungle, but only one main road. There are numerous homes off the main road, but many are vacant most of the year. We're doing what we can to check out each and every home, but to be honest, there are very few law enforcement officers on the island."

The new man typed feverishly on the computer controlling the large flat screen.

"At four forty-five this morning, this video arrived in the President's secure email." Branson nodded toward the man who flicked a few keys.

A black man with an extremely large lower lip held a gun to the head of a dark-haired woman in a dirty tank top and what looked like silk running shorts. "Mr. President, I am Lynda Thompson, Senator Carl Thompson's wife." Her voice cracked on almost every word as her body shook. "We've met several times." Her eyes moved as though she were reading cue cards, then quickly darted to the side. "I have a message from...Aaa... hill," she struggled with the word.

The man looked directly into the camera lens and lifted his chin. Rayne felt like she was looking into the eyes of pure evil. "You know who I am." He spoke in clear English with a slight British accent. "I am Aahil Mohamed Jaja." His snide smile held a secret.

He jerked his head to the side and the camera panned

slowly across his captives. Two other women were tied back-to-back, gagged with dirty bandannas.

"The curly-haired brunette is Rita Garcia and she is tied to the girls' teacher, Annamarie Rogers," Branson announced.

Their pleading eyes almost broke Rayne's heart, just before panic struck.

Where the hell was Angelique Sedgwick? The new wife of the Speaker of the House had decided hours before Callie was to leave on the fall break trip that the Caribbean would be a great place to shop. Against the advice of Rayne's Secret Service team, the persistent woman had packed several bags, and jumped into the limousine provided for their family's security. She'd trotted in four-inch heels and a designer sundress, behind her stepdaughter and boarded the private jet, uninvited.

Rayne wished she had a picture of the new Mrs. Sedgwick's face as she rolled her bags through the sand and saw the tents for the first time. Rayne knew she shouldn't think so little of Angelique Sedgwick, but she had adored Bette, the first wife.

"Take a good look at who I have." Jaja bragged. Two men carrying automatic rifles crossed the screen as they paced in front of the frightened women and children.

"Slow down the video," Branson ordered. He opened up his file and started shuffling through photographs. "I think the first one is Violet Russell. Next to her, that looks to be...Sophia Edwards."

"No, sir, that's Luna Collins," Rayne corrected before she could stop herself.

Branson looked down the table at her. "Can you identify all these girls?"

"Yes. I watched them grow up over the last three

years. They've all been in the Sedgwick home multiple times." Rayne said with confidence.

"Please, tell everyone else seated here so we can start to memorize their faces and names." It was an order, and everyone gathered there knew it.

Rayne took a deep breath. "Just to repeat, the first young girl is Violet Russell. Next to her is Luna Collins. Gia," she corrected herself, "Gianna Mason, then Sophia Edwards. That's Callie Sedgwick holding Charlotte Thompson on one side and Brynn Olesen on the other."

It was just like Callie to be the one to soothe her friend or defend her if necessary. The little blond-haired twelve-year-old had an old soul. While watching her mother slowly die of cancer, the young lady—and she was a lady at heart—had always greeted her mother with an encouraging smile and a hug. The child somehow knew that was exactly what her mother needed.

Now this had happened to that poor little girl.

Rayne had to do everything in her power to get Callie out of Jaja's clutches.

Refocusing, she continued, "Aria Moore, Elianna Martin, and the last one is Zoey Garcia. We saw her mother tied to Ms. Rogers."

Just as Rayne was about to point out that Angelique Sedgwick was missing, the camera jerked as though someone was walking away from the others. The woman in question appeared by herself, in a corner. She tried to talk around several bandannas stuffed into her mouth and another holding them in place tied behind her head. She seemed to be screaming *Let me go*. When she realized she was on video, the words sounded as though she was saying *No, no, no one can see me like this*, as she hunched her shoulders and tried to bury her face in the corner.

Rayne grimaced. That was so much like Angelique Sedgwick, more concerned about her personal appearance and what other people thought than the health and safety of her stepdaughter.

As the cameraman turned, the video was almost dizzying until it stopped back on Jaja and Lynda Thompson.

"Mr. President, all-powerful and secure in your White House, you have now seen who I have. I want you to think about it for a while. I'll be back in touch with you, soon." The screen went black.

Rayne returned her gaze to the head of the table. It looked as though the new man was staring at her but his face was hidden in shadow. Maybe he didn't get all the names of the girls in order, or perhaps he needed more details. They could catch up after the meeting.

"Every frame of this video is being analyzed," Branson announced. "We just wanted you to see what you're dealing with. We'll be updating the rescue team on the flight. There is no airport on St. John so you'll be flying into St. Thomas where you will be picked up by U.S. Navy helicopters. We are fortunate that the USS *Abraham Lincoln*, and its escort of cruisers and destroyers, are in international waters off Venezuela. We'll have more details before you land."

"Director Brandon, do we have a firm location of the hostages?" a man across the table asked.

Shaking his head, the task force chairman explained, "We are currently moving satellites to cover the area. We'll use thermal imaging when possible, but until the officers on the ground check out every house, we don't have anything to go by. The Rangers have told us there are three other large groups; two from churches containing mostly high school juniors and seniors, and a troop of Boy Scouts. They have been ordered to remain in camp until further notice. Hopefully we'll have an update while you're in the air."

"Can someone, please, get the lights?" The man at the computer stood, turning his back to those at the table and spoke quietly with Mr. Branson. Rayne mentally corrected herself, *Director* Branson. She stared at the man who set off alarms in her head. Her senses weren't screaming danger—more like a storm that had been upgraded from a warning to an advisory, meaning bad shit was headed your way.

When the lights came on, she was looking at her briefing book to see if she knew anyone on the task force. None of the names sounded familiar. Glancing around the group, she was happy to see three other women.

Director Branson nodded once then scanned everyone's faces. "We have an addition to the task force and the rescue team. She is the Senior Special Agent in charge of Congressman Robert Sedgwick's Secret Service detail and is well-acquainted with Aahil Mohammed Jaja after working in that agency's North African office for several years. Please welcome Rayne Yoshida."

She felt kind of odd having everyone's attention focused on her.

Greetings of "Welcome" and "Thanks for joining us" echoed around the table as some of the men gave her a nod.

The man next to Director Branson whipped around and glared at Rayne.

Her stomach flipped over, and her breakfast started to crawl up her throat. She swallowed hard, fighting the urge to throw up.

"For those of you who didn't meet him at the earlier briefing, this is Dex Carson. He'll be leading the rescue team." Branson slid his gaze to Dex. "He, too, had a run-in with Jaja back when he commanded a SEAL team."

Rayne couldn't take her eyes off Dex. He had aged well. She liked the gray at his temples and sprinkling through his dark brown hair. The cut hadn't changed, though. He still wore it tight to his head, perhaps a little longer on top these days. The full beard was gone, though, replaced by a neatly trimmed, very graying patch of hair that started as a mustache and ended under his chin, encircling those full lips that had kissed every inch of her naked body. He'd rolled up his camouflage shirt sleeves, exposing cut biceps and forearms. If they were any indication, he had remained quite fit.

Damn. He was still so fucking handsome, but that was one place she would never go with him, again.

He had nearly ruined her career. She would never forgive him for that.

"Dex, good luck." Director Branson slapped him on the shoulder. "Happy hunting."

"My team will meet in ten minutes at the vehicles," Dex announced, then strode directly toward Rayne, who had finished gathering her briefing book and stood.

He scowled as he raked his gaze slowly over her black jacket, down her starched white blouse, to the matching pants. He gaped at her two-inch pumps and shook his head.

Without lifting his gaze, he suggested, "Why don't you do us both a favor and coordinate things from here? You're not even dressed for this operation and we are ready to leave."

Not just no, but fuck no. He was not going to bulldoze

over her. She didn't get the position as the head of the Secret Service detail for the Speaker of the House by allowing men to change her orders at the last-minute. Besides, she could slip out of these clothes and into camouflage in less than three minutes. Five, if it included lacing up her boots which she could easily fasten while in route.

"I am here as an active member of this team." Rayne was frustrated when he didn't meet her gaze. Accustomed to reluctant men, she used her command voice, "Look at me when I speak to you."

Dex slowly raised his head as though in defiance. The muscle in the side of his jaw was jumping when his eyes met hers. "You are not in charge of this operation, thank Christ. I am."

Oh. He was not going to go there. Not now. Not ever. Although they hadn't captured Jaja, that mission had been extremely successful.

She knew she had to play nice. "Rescuing Callie Sedgwick is my primary assignment. Making sure her stepmother gets home safely is my secondary duty." Rayne let out a long sigh. "I know all these children, personally. There is no one here who wants to save these girls more than me."

"Are you going to be able to take orders from me?" His question seemed to pound into her chest while his deep brown eyes never left hers. "Or are you going to fight me on everything?"

"You're the team commander," she admitted.

Satisfaction gleamed in his eyes.

"But I will offer my opinion whenever I think it's necessary." That was part of her training and experience.

His jaw muscle flexed.

"If there's nothing else, Commander Carson, I need to change into jungle cammies." Without waiting for his permission, Rayne walked over and grabbed her bag. She'd seen the ladies' room down the hall. She could do this. "I'll meet you at the vehicles."

"If you're not there in six minutes, we're not waiting for you," Dex warned.

Five minutes later, Rayne placed her bag next to the others in the back of an SUV. "With minutes to spare," she bragged as she walked by Dex and crawled into the backseat.

Hidden from his view, she let out a long slow breath. None of this was going to be easy.

CHAPTER THREE

Callie was hungry.

And thirsty.

And hot.

Her arms also ached. She had been holding Charlotte for hours, or so it seemed. When Acne Face and Grunt— the names Callie had mentally given the guards—had untied Mrs. Thompson and threw her at Jaja, her best friend yelled and screamed at the bad men to leave her mother alone.

Callie knew that was the wrong thing to do, so she grabbed Charlotte. While she hugged her friend, she whispered in her ear, telling her everything would be all right, and she didn't want the bad men to take notice of her.

They had done everything that Mr. Jaja told them to do since his men had ripped open their tents and wrapped them in their sheets. Callie knew his name thanks to him constantly repeating it for the camera. She only wished that she had her cell phone with her, but there hadn't been time to grab it. Otherwise, she would have already Googled this jerk.

Or texted a message to her dad. She wondered if he had seen the video. Her heart squeezed. She wondered if he even cared. Since he married the Barbie wannabe, Callie sometimes wondered if her dad had forgotten all about her. When school was out, she tried to spend as much time with her friends as possible. She couldn't bear to be in that house with the step witch. She had changed everything.

The warm kitchen with cherry cabinets that nearly reached the tall ceiling, and golden granite countertops where she and her mom had baked cookies and often made supper together, was now twice the size. The new, stainless steel appliances, gray walls and white cabinets were as cold as Her Highness the Wicked Witch, who couldn't make anything for dinner except reservations at the most expensive restaurants in DC. Cooking would be too close to food and she might be tempted to sample a bite and gain an ounce.

It was a darn good thing that her father had listened when she complained that there was literally no food in the house, then showed him an empty refrigerator. In front of her dad, Step-Momzilla had put on a big show of giving a crap about her new daughter. She then ordered all Callie's favorite foods over the Internet and had them delivered. Later, when she and Step-Momster were alone, the woman set up an account online so Callie could order anything her little heart, and belly, ever wanted. That was probably the nicest thing the woman had ever done for her.

Thinking of food just made her even more hungry. Glancing around the room, she took in her friends seated against the inside wall of the empty house. The only noise was an occasional sniff or whimper from one of her friends and the clunk of heavy boots as the guards walked back and forth in front of them. As though any of them were stupid enough to try to get up and run away.

As soon as she had that thought, cranky Angelique's ignorant display popped into her mind. The minute they had untied Queen Bitch from her seat, Non-Mom had bolted for the door, concerned about no one but herself. She deserved to be put in the corner like a recalcitrant child.

Even though the blinds were drawn, and the drapes pulled over them, Callie had seen daylight for hours. She wondered if they were going to starve them to death. She also speculated whether you died first of starvation or dehydration.

Brynn peeked around Charlotte and barely whispered, "I have to pee really bad. I mean, *really* bad. Do you think they'd let me go?" Brynn grimaced and darted her eyes toward the guards. "I think I started my period."

"Crap." The mouthed word escaped before Callie could hold it in.

"No. I didn't poop my pants." Brynn scrunched her nose and covertly pointed toward the guard. "I think he did though. Maybe it's just bad gas, but he stinks."

Charlotte and Brynn carefully nodded their heads in agreement.

Callie stared at Ms. Rogers, hoping to mentally connect to her teacher, or at least catch her eye. When their gazes finally met, she mouthed *potty*. At the confused faces of all three women, Callie tried, *bathroom*.

When that didn't work, she put her hand over her bladder and splayed her fingers out several times.

Did she start her period? Mrs. Thompson mouthed.

Callie nodded and let out a long sigh. She had learned to kind-of read lips during the last few months as her mother was losing her battle against cancer and could barely talk. Even though it had been over two years, Callie still had to fight back tears. She missed her mother so much.

Blinking hard to clear her blurry eyes, Callie watched the three adult women sitting together quietly discuss the situation.

"Mr. Jaja, would you please consider untying me so I could tend to the girls?" Ms. Rogers was really brave. She was pretty awesome, especially for a teacher. Even more awesome as their Girl Scout leader. She knew how to camp and everything. "Maybe I can get them some water? Or something to eat? They probably have to go to the bathroom, too."

Callie just stared at Mr. Jaja, watching his every move, hoping Ms. Rogers didn't make him mad, like her Step-Monster had. Moving as little as possible, Callie bent her head ever so slightly to look over at the Dragon Lady stuffed in the far corner. In a way, she felt bad for the woman who had married her dad. God just hadn't seen fit to give that woman many brains. She was an idiot, bless her heart.

Angelique had yelled at their captors, called them ugly names, so they had stuffed all those rags in her mouth. After the video, they didn't gag Mrs. Thompson or tie her up again, but made her sit with Ms. Rogers and Mrs. Garcia, Zoe's mom. Eventually, Mrs. Thompson convinced Mr. Jaja that the other women would be quiet if they took the gags off. That worked for everyone except callused Angelique. The minute they even loosened her gag she started screaming at them, again. The woman never learned.

All their kidnappers started talking at once and Callie snapped her gaze to see if Ms. Rogers was okay. She was. Relief washed through her.

One of their two guards left the big living room in the empty house. Jaja strolled in front of the girls and they all cowered against the wall, trying to make themselves as small as possible. Sophia burst into quiet tears. When they had arrived, it had taken nearly an hour for her to stop crying. Gia, Violet, and Luna all took turns to comfort her. Sophia was a big crybaby anyway. Callie was pretty sure the girl did it for the attention. Her mom and dad were going through a divorce and things were rough for her at home.

Jaja seemed to size up each girl. Callie didn't like the way that man watched them. Well, in truth, she didn't like the way *any* of the men looked at her friends and their chaperones. There was something about their faces that just didn't feel right. They just completely creeped her out.

Huffing out a breath after he passed her, she scrutinized the leader as he approached Ms. Rogers. "You may escort each girl to the bathroom." Jaja pointed down the hall. "The door must stay open and you must stay with the girl. Stand in the hall where I can see you." He pointed to Mrs. Thompson. "You, come with me."

Callie whispered in Charlotte's ear, "Don't say a word. Your mother is fine. She's helping them. Do you understand?"

Her best friend nodded.

Ms. Rogers stood in front of the ten girls. "Is there anyone who has to take care of their female problems?"

Brynn's hand shot into the air. "Me," she squealed quietly.

After looking up and down the row, Ms. Rogers signaled to Brynn, who rolled to her knees and gave her a hug. "Thanks, Callie. I was too scared to tell anyone."

Their teacher threw her arm around Brynn's shoulders and whispered something into her ear. Ms. Rogers knew who had already started their monthly cycles and who hadn't. At an all-girls school, getting your period was a rite of passage.

Callie, who had only turned twelve three months ago, was a late bloomer. She barely had boobs. In truth, she really didn't need to wear a bra yet, but she did because everyone else in her class had been wearing them for nearly a year. Some even longer.

It was finally Callie's turn to use the restroom.

"Everything is going to be okay," Ms. Rogers reassured her as they walked with their arms around each other to the bathroom. After she had washed her hands, she cupped them together into a bowl and gathered water so she could drink. She hadn't realized how thirsty she was until she had emptied her makeshift cup for the third time. She then used the water to wash her face and arms. She really wanted to step into the shower and change out of her pajamas. Although she was fully covered, she felt half naked.

Glancing down the hall, she saw two more rooms, probably bedrooms. She wondered if there was a master bedroom where the mom and dad stayed, and if they had two children who had lived in those bedrooms and shared that bathroom. Not for the first time, she wondered what it would be like to have a sibling.

Ms. Rogers threw her arm around Callie once again. "Thank you for taking care of Charlotte. I know she's scared. I know you all are. I'm going to see if Mr. Jaja will let me talk to all of you together for just a few minutes after everyone is done using the restroom." She dropped her arm and signaled for Charlotte to come next.

Everyone had been allowed a visit to the bathroom, including the moms—although Callie didn't consider Angelique as a mom, they had even allowed her to go under the guidance of Ms. Rogers. Callie wondered what her teacher had whispered in Barbie's ear. Hopefully, she read her the riot act, and maybe, just maybe, the woman would pull her crap together and act like an adult. Callie did find it amusing, though, that their kidnappers would not un-gag her stepmother.

After a quiet conversation between Ms. Rogers and Mr. Jaja, her teacher called all the girls into a circle. Mrs. Thompson grabbed Charlotte and hugged her tight as did Mrs. Garcia with Zoey.

"Mr. Jaja wants to thank you all for cooperating. If we continue to do as he instructs, we can continue to have some freedom in this room. We all need to thank Mrs. Thompson for being so brave to make the video for Mr. Jaja." She clapped and everyone followed her lead. She glanced over her shoulder and the leader nodded his head in approval and agreement.

"You all remember our active shooter drills at school?" At the teacher's question, everyone nodded their heads. It was a drill they were forced to practice every year. Since they had gone to the same school for at least five years together, they all knew what to do.

"Excellent." Ms. Rogers clapped her hands and gave them a genuine smile. "I'd say this qualifies." She tilted her head toward the armed guards. "So, let's review what we do in an active shooter situation."

Eager hands went into the air.

She called on Elianna. "We sit quietly and don't say a word."

"Yes. Exactly." Ms. Rogers looked around for someone else to call on. "Violet."

"Can we use the bathroom rather than a bucket like we have at school?"

Ms. Rogers started to answer then looked at Mr. Jaja, who simply dipped his chin. "As long as all of us are good, we can continue to use the bathroom." Another glance toward their primary captor confirmed her words.

Sighs echoed in the two-story room.

"What are some of the other things we do in active shooter situation?" Ms. Rogers repeated the question then called on Aria.

"We're supposed to turn off the ringers on our cell phones, but we don't have them." She glared at their captors.

"You are correct on both counts. Who else can give me some of the rules?" Their teacher then called on Gia.

"We're supposed to stay in our hiding place until law enforcement gives us the all clear." Gia gave everyone a small smile.

"You are absolutely right. So, we might be here a while until we get the all clear, and Mr. Jaja lets us go home." When Mrs. Rogers looked at the leader, Callie could tell her smile was forced.

"Now, do you remember when Luna's mom came in and talked to us on career day?" At all the head nods, she continued, "What are we supposed to do in the case of a kidnapping?"

"We're not supposed to argue or make them mad," Aria said.

All heads turned toward the corner where Callie's stepmother was wedged between the two walls, watching intently. "Callie's mom is doing everything you're not supposed to do," Aria pointed out unnecessarily.

"She's not my mother," Callie snapped. "She's just a bimbo my dad married because he missed my mom so much." All the women and girls, except for Step Monster, had been part of the support system for both Callie and her mom as she lost her two-year battle to cancer. She knew these women had her back.

Angelique Sedgwick glared daggers at her stepdaughter. Callie doubted she'd get in trouble for telling the truth. But if looks could kill, she'd certainly be dead.

"Perhaps Mrs. Sedgwick now understands what she should do, and what she should *not* do." At her teacher's suggestion, everyone looked at the woman trussed up in the corner.

Angelique Sedgwick nodded.

Everyone's head turned then to Mr. Jaja. "If she keeps her mouth shut, we won't have to gag her." His eyes ran up and down her barely-there nighty. The man's grin made Callie's empty stomach curdle. "Yes, untie her, too. She can sit with the other women now."

Mrs. Thompson and Mrs. Garcia went over and released her stepmother from her bonds.

The woman who had married her father leaped out of the corner, fingers curled like claws, as she sprinted toward Mr. Jaja. "How dare you treat me like this? Do you know who my husband is? I need a cell phone. I'm entitled to a call."

Mr. Jaja burst out laughing. "Listen you little bitch, you're not under arrest in the United States. You've. Been. Kidnapped. There is no one here who is going to give you a fucking cell phone to call anyone."

He snapped his fingers and the two guards grabbed her.

Mr. Jaja walked slowly to her, but kept far enough away so she couldn't kick him as she wiggled, trying to get free. He stepped around his guard and grabbed her bleach-blond hair and pulled back, so she was facing the ceiling. "I don't like a smart mouth on a woman. Her mouth should be used for sucking dick."

Both guards chuckled and nodded in agreement.

Mr. Jaja stared at her huge fake boobs. "Maybe I'll keep you gagged and fuck you hard just to show you what it's like to be with a real man before I let you go."

"Don't you dare touch me you vile—"

Mr. Jaja backhanded her and she slumped unconscious. She was tied up, gagged, and back in the corner within a minute.

Callie leaned forward and buried her head in her hands. *Idiot! She's going to get someone killed.*

CHAPTER FOUR

As soon as the customized Homeland Security jet reached cruising altitude, Dex unbuckled and stood at the head of the aisle. He took in the face of each of his new team members and realized that he didn't know any of them.

Well, that was a lie. The one member of his team that he knew very well, intimately, was the last person in the world he wanted on that plane. Rayne Yoshida. He found his gaze lingering on her, assessing her, but not as a team leader. As a man.

She was still so pretty. Her black hair was pulled back in a tight bun at the nape of her neck. He wondered how long it had grown. Twelve years ago, it had tickled his thighs and draped over his hips when she had taken him into her mouth. The soft strands brushed his shoulders as she had ridden him, taking them both to a height he'd never experienced before...or since.

Her triangular face had always fascinated him. A high, still-smooth forehead was a hint to her intelligence. Perfectly arched eyebrows help define her large cat eyes that swept up at the corners, indicative of the Japanese heritage on her mother's side. Although her eyes were primarily brown, gold and green flecks dominated their color when she was aroused.

All he saw in them now was contempt, or maybe that was simply determination.

Her chiseled cheekbones were defined by a square jaw that came to a pointed chin. For Dex, though, it was those beautiful plump lips that had touched his body everywhere that made his cock stand up and pay attention. They were so soft, giving, not demanding. So much like Rayne herself, in the bedroom. On the job, the woman was a ballbuster.

Tearing his gaze from her once again, he surveyed his new team.

He would start with the two Navy SEALs provided by the State Department. He signaled for them to join him at the table he'd sequestered upfront.

"Ethan Steadman." The first man held out his hand. "Call me Blade."

"You good with one?" Dex had often given his men their handle after some incident on a mission.

"Yeah." The single word and a grin were his answer.

"Liam Bridger. Shep to most." His handshake was firm but not bone-crushing.

"Okay, I have to ask, why Shep?" Dex was always curious how everyone got their nicknames.

Liam gave him a small grin. "A herd of sheep in the mountains of Afghanistan became the best cover we could find. Some of our city boys didn't have a clue. Shepherd stuck for a while, then everybody just shortened it to Shep."

"That a Wyoming accent I detect?" Dex had gotten good about identifying accents.

"That's one of the places we lived. Montana, Idaho, Colorado, we moved around a lot." Liam had lost his smile.

"Long way from deep blue water," Dex stated.

The smile was back. "Yep."

"Gentlemen, call me Dex, my name. My handle, my trident, and uniforms all got packed away when I retired a year ago." Both men gave him a chin lift. He tapped the personnel folders in front of him. "Tell me what's not in here and why you're on this team."

"I got tired of the bullshit. One of my teammates got out a few months before I was eligible and went to work for a Beltway bandit with State Department contracts." Blade told a story that Dex had heard a dozen times from the men at Guardian Security. "The money was three times what I was earning as an E-5. I'm not stupid." He tapped the file with his index finger. "I was a damn good SEAL. I've been on *lots* of raid and rescues, including a few in West Africa."

"Good." At least the State Department vetted that one. His gaze went to Shep.

"Same story, except I was a West Coast SEAL. Most of my rescues were in Southeast Asia, hot, steamy, fucking jungles." He tilted his head toward Blade. "We work for the same contractor."

Dex took a deep breath. "Look, men, we all come from the same training and experience so I'm going to depend very heavily on you two. I'll be using standard SEAL hand signals and will be approaching this situation the same way I would any other kidnapping or hostage mission if this were a SEAL team."

Both men nodded once. After discussing their weapons, Dex started to feel much better about this op.

"Thank you, men. You may want to review the hostage pictures and the video so we can identify each one." Dex stood, signaling they were excused. Just as he was about to invite the two women from the FBI, his phone rang.

He swiped to accept the call and sat back down. "Hello, Alex. Thank you again for understanding that I'll be unavailable until this mission is completed." He grinned. "And thanks for all the special toys."

"You're welcome." The smile in Alex's voice came through the line. "I just wanted you to know that we've been contacted by the president of the girls' school board and hired to assist...if needed."

Dex was about to thank his boss and tell him additional assistance wasn't needed, but he quickly reconsidered and concluded that additional backup might prove necessary given there were fourteen hostages. "Thank you. Let's hope we don't need any more firepower."

"I explained to them that because the kidnappers were not Americans, this became an international situation, but assured them that one of our men was leading the team under the Department of Homeland Security." Alex went on to say, "I'm going to pull together the same team we used in Venezuela since you're accustomed to working with them. We're going to stage on St. Thomas. I've secured a house there for us to use and a couple vehicles, including a boat if needed."

"I'll be sure to stay in touch." Dex briefly wondered what the Department of Homeland Security would think about him bringing on an outside team, then he swept the worry away. He really didn't care. It was nice to be able to do what was necessary for the mission.

"I'll let you know when we've established our base on St. Thomas. Stay safe, Dex." Alex hung up.

Yes. Dex was feeling better about this mission every minute. He stood and signaled to the two women who sat together about halfway back.

"Senior Special Agent Vanessa Overholt," the one with curly hair that was more silver than black said as she firmly shook his hand.

"Special Agent Tonya Fields." Dex wondered how old she was because in his opinion she didn't look a day over twenty-two and he knew that you had to be twenty-six to get into the FBI. He hoped this wasn't her first op.

As he sat down, Vanessa immediately informed him, "We are both specialists in kidnapping, and this isn't our first dance. Our instructions are to set up on St. Thomas and care for the women and girls as soon as you bring them to us." Vanessa folded her hands and rested her forearms on the table. "I'm not sure what to call you other than sir."

Dex was glad he had a moment to speak. "My name is Dex and please don't call me sir. No one on this team has a rank, but we all have a job to do." He smiled then. "And I'm glad you spelled everything you intend to do out to me. You said you've done this before. Have you handled this many hostages at one time?"

"No, and that's what I was going to speak to you about next." Vanessa certainly was direct, and given their short time frame, Dex appreciated it. "Do you have a problem with me calling in additional hostage specialists? I can have them on the next flight. The agency is sending a team of physicians and nurses within twelve hours to establish a clinic. Each of the hostages is going to need a complete physical and a psychological exam. Our protocol requires that we do that before allowing them to return home."

"Sounds like a plan," Dex admitted. "Make your calls. I want to see that these hostages get the best care possible. Keep in mind that they're being held by an Islamic extremist who has absolutely no respect for women, especially Christians, and since we have no idea what is being said to them and in front of them, religious issues may need to be addressed."

Standing, Dex added, "Let me know what else you need. At this point, I don't believe we're going to be denied anything."

"I could use a raise," Vanessa quipped. Her smile transformed her no-nonsense demeanor into one of a caring woman. "If you're serious, I'll make a list."

"We can ask. All they can do is say no." He smiled then, remembering Alex's words. "I have access to some outside funding for this mission that we may be able to tap."

Her eyebrows lifted as did the corners of her mouth. "In that case, give me fifteen minutes and you'll have a list."

Dex nodded then grinned. "Don't bother putting a raise on that list. I can't make that happen. Anything else, though, we'll see."

Vanessa practically marched down the aisle, but Tonya lingered. "This is my twelfth kidnapping. I know I look young, but I'm thirty-two, and I have a PhD in child psychology focusing on teens. I use my youthful appearance to my advantage. Young girls relate to me." She glanced down toward her feet before raising her eyes to meet his. "I know exactly what these girls are going through. I was raised Muslim and promised from birth. My parents escaped from Iran when I was a child, but that didn't stop my husband from claiming me when I was twelve. When he discovered I had become a Christian and attended Catholic school most of my life, he rejected me and returned me to my parents...eventually."

Dex couldn't miss the resolve that had taken over her entire body as she stood straighter and squared her shoulders. "I understand men like Aahil Mohammed Jaja and know how quickly they can damage a child's self-worth. That's why I am on this team."

Pride, revulsion, and a dozen other emotions ran through Dex at the same time. He held out his hand and she took it, but they didn't shake. He simply held it. "I'm glad you're here. I believe you are uniquely qualified to handle this situation." He released her hand.

"Just get them to us as quickly as possible." Tonya turned and walked to her seat where she and Vanessa immediately jumped into conversation.

After checking the time, Dex strode to the quad seating near the back of the plane where the four men from the Department of Justice sat playing cards, as though this were a ride to their favorite vacation spot.

When he was six feet away, he heard one of them say, "Our turn."

They immediately turned the cards upside down onto the table.

Dex slid into the single seat across from them and swung the comfortable captain's chair to face all four. He took a brief moment to study the faces of the former Green Berets. He'd memorized their files.

"If you don't mind, I'm going to speak to you as a

group rather than individually." Dex received a nod from each man. "I was a Navy SEAL, so we have similar training. Two years ago, before I retired, I was the commanding officer of a SEAL Team, which is about twice the size of your Army company. Bottom line, we all worked for USSOCOM. But none of us wear a uniform anymore, so I expect you to call me Dex. I don't want anybody to call me sir."

He got silent nods once again.

Grinning, he added, "And I expect you to play nice with the two SEALS upfront. As of this moment, we're all on the same team with one goal in mind, rescue fourteen hostages."

Again, a single chin dip from each man.

"William Edge." Dex was pretty sure he looked at the correct man.

"That's me." Raking his fingers through his long blond hair, he looked a lot like Chris Hemsworth in Thor. "Call me Will."

"You got it, Will." Dex slid his gaze to the man beside him. "Stephen Clayborn?"

"Steve," he said with a nod. His neatly trimmed dark brown hair and beard were such a contrast to Will.

"I understand the two of you are specially trained medics." At their nod, he continued, "In the video it didn't look like anyone was hurt, but as we all know that can change in a heartbeat. I want you two in the second wave through the door." One corner of Dex's mouth kicked up. "Devin Martindale. Robert Taylor." He looked at the men on the other side of the table. "You're with me on the breach."

The two men high-fived each other with big smiles.

"Kickin' ass," Robert exclaimed.

"We don't need their fucking names," Devon added.

"Any asshole who kidnaps little girls deserves to die," Will chimed in.

"I'd love to be the one to put a bullet through Jaja's forehead," Steve proclaimed.

Devon looked at his teammate smugly. "We get first dibs at him since we're the first bullet catchers."

Dex enjoyed their playful banter. "How long have you guys worked together?"

Robert dramatically looked at his watch. "Long time. Almost seven hours."

"Department of Justice didn't send me an existing team?" Dex didn't know if he was more surprised or pissed.

"No." The men had spoken in unison. They already functioned as a cohesive team.

"We're used to operating this way," Robert explained. "DOJ picks who they think is necessary for that mission, announces who's in charge, and throws us on a plane. We usually get briefed in the air."

"Yeah, the meeting this morning was awesome. We never get that level of big picture." Will smiled. He pointed to the stack of briefing files. "Those are really detailed compared to what we're normally given."

Dex looked at the pile with concern.

"Don't worry, Dex, we've got them memorized," Robert assured him.

"Good." He glanced toward the front and whistled. "Blade. Shep." He signaled for the SEALs to come to the back. Turning his attention back to the Green Berets, he announced, "Time to play nice."

As soon as the other two men got within earshot, he announced to his breaching team, "These two are going to teach you the hand signals I'll be using. Poker is the new game. Deal them in. By the time we land in St. Thomas, I'm looking for you to be a solid team at my back."

Dex walked away, leaving the younger men to fight it out or become friends. He bet on the latter outcome.

He was going to slide into the seat beside Rayne and talk to her, but his phone rang. When he checked the caller ID, he didn't recognize the number.

"Dex Carson."

"Please hold for Captain Fortney of the USS *Abraham Lincoln*."

Dex had answered many calls like this before when he wore a Navy uniform.

"Commander Carson, this is Captain John Fortney, commanding officer of the USS *Abraham Lincoln*. The admiral has instructed me to support you in any way possible. I have been briefed on your mission. We have four Seahawks preparing to head to St. Thomas Island." The man's voice changed from rapid-fire briefing to one of concern. "What else can I do to help you, Commander?"

Dex wasn't going to waste time correcting the captain's assumption that he was still active duty.

Doubting that they were on a secure line, Dex asked, "I have a real hankering for frogs legs. Any chance you have some on board that you might be willing to send my way?"

"I have plenty," the captain replied. Dex was pleased that the man had understood he was asking for SEALs.

"If you could have them delivered to the little island, I'm sure the five men in uniform there would truly appreciate some frog legs."

The captain laughed. "I think I can make that happen."

"Thank you, sir."

"By the way, Commander Carson, we're watching a storm developing off Africa. It's currently only a tropical depression, but some of the weather guessers think it could go big."

Christ. Another thing Dex had to worry about. The tick-tock of time seemed to surround him.

"Thanks for the information, sir. I'll have Washington start tracking that."

"Good hunting. The *Abraham Lincoln* out." The line went dead.

Dex quickly typed out a note about the impending weather conditions and sent it to Si Branson. Hopefully, it would fizzle out and die at sea.

As he looked at his stack of personnel files, he knew who he had to go see next. Part of him wanted to go to her since she was surrounded by other members of the team. He was sure she wouldn't bring up anything personal within earshot of someone else. But that was the cowardly way out. He was a SEAL and had never backed down from adversity.

Dex took a deep breath and stood before making an uninterrupted line for her seat.

"We need to talk."

She pointed to the chair beside her, obviously reluctant as well.

Dex flipped his thumb toward the front. "Privately." Without waiting for her reply, he turned on his heel and strode to his seat.

CHAPTER FIVE

Point to Dex. Not that Rayne was actually keeping count as she made her way to his table at the very front of the plane. So, he didn't want to talk where anyone else could overhear them. On the other hand, he had talked to the others privately so why should she be any different?

He signaled for her to sit across from him. "You'll be staying on St. Thomas with the FBI women." It was a statement, not a question.

"No. I'll be on the breaching team." She hoped her voice would have been softer, but Rayne had never been good at hiding her feelings.

Dex narrowed his eyes. "That's my call, not yours."

"The women from the FBI have a completely different mission than I do. Callie and Angelique Sedgwick are my responsibility. I'm going in to get them," she insisted. "And if Jaja gets in my way, he's going down along with everyone else who dared to kidnap those children." She hadn't meant to pause, so she quickly added, "and the four women."

"I'm in charge of this team and you'll do what I tell

you to do." Dex leaned forward and put his forearms on the table.

Rayne was not going to be intimidated by that tactic. She had gone to the same Navy Officers Candidate School as Dex. Then she had additional training at Judge Advocate School before working in the JAG office as an investigator, even though she had a law degree. She'd always preferred to be the one kicking down doors. After completing her tour in the Navy, she'd been recruited as an investigator for the Secret Service because she was damn good at her job.

Until she had literally fucked up one night with the hunk of testosterone sitting across from her.

She couldn't go there now. She had to rescue Callie... and the Speaker's wife.

To counter his move, she mirrored it by placing her forearms on the table and leaning forward as well.

"This is a joint task force and I am the Secret Service representative. I will be there to rescue Callie and Angelique." Without realizing it, Rayne had moved even closer until her nose was only two inches from Dex's. Aware of their closeness, but unwilling to back off, she held her position and stared into eyes the color of good whiskey.

"I see you're still the ballbuster you were twelve years ago." Dex straightened his back as he sat up.

Once again, she mirrored his move. "I didn't get to be the highest-ranking woman in personal protection by allowing misogynistic men to walk all over me."

His eyebrows pinched together. "I thought you're on the investigative side?"

Damn. She did not want to talk about this. But maybe it was time he learned how badly he had damaged her career. "I had to switch career paths eleven years ago after I was finally cleared of any wrongdoing in Nigeria if I wanted to stay with the Secret Service." She glared at him. "I like working for this agency and didn't want to give up my job."

She noticed her name on the personnel file in front of him and tapped it with her index finger. "I'm sure everything you need to know is in there." She spread her arms wide. "I can assure you I have kept in top physical condition, a requirement for my job." She started to stand up. "Now, Commander Carson, unless you have specific questions for me concerning this mission, I'll just return to my seat."

"Sit down," he ordered sharply.

She debated just turning and leaving but thought better of it. She was expected to be a team player and he was the team leader, no matter how much she hated that fact. She had given him her word that she would follow his orders.

When his gaze met hers, his eyes softened. "Please."

She settled back into the plush captain's chair. As the Speaker of the House, Robert Sedgwick was given first-class treatment everywhere he went. Even though she had become accustomed to executive jets, she had to admit that this one was exceptionally nice.

"First, it's no longer Commander Carson."

That was a shock. When they had worked together over a decade before, Dex had wanted to make a career out of the Navy, the lifer kind where they were going to have to throw him out after thirty years.

Her heart beat faster. Had he been dishonorably discharged after the Nigeria incident? No. She had cleared his name, even though he hadn't done the same for her. She had proven to the investigators that Dex had nothing to do with the hookers.

Had something else gone wrong during the years that followed?

"It's now just Dex. I retired over a year ago," he explained.

She quickly did the math and realized he had been in the Navy for twenty years, the requirement for retirement. Rayne still wondered why he had left the job he had always loved. Maybe, like her, his career path had to change.

He brought her back to the present and the situation at hand. "I need you to talk to me about these little girls."

Rayne didn't consider Callie and her friends as 'little girls.' Young ladies, yes.

"Do you think that each man on the breaching team could carry two girls to safety?" He cocked his elbows out to the side as though he were holding small children.

"No. I don't believe they can."

Shock washed over his face. "Have you seen the size of the men on this team?"

"Yes. But I also know the size of these girls." She tried to explain, "At twelve and thirteen years old, they've reached their adult height. They are all between five foot four inches and five foot nine."

Dex's eyebrows shot up.

"These are young *ladies*, not little children." She indicated the height difference with her hand. "It was very difficult to see their true size in the video, but I can assure you, Gia is five foot nine and she's thirteen years old. She's also a competitive diver hoping to make it to the Junior Olympics this year."

"Okay, so she could hold her own in the jungle, as

long as she's not hurt." Dex pulled out the list of names of the hostages and placed a check mark beside Gianna. "What about the rest of these girls?"

It was a good thing Rayne could read upside down because she didn't want to get close to him and share the piece of paper.

"I've seen these girls in action. They are far from helpless." She pointed to Luna Collins's name. "She has a brown belt in karate and she's one tough young lady. Her mom works for the FBI as a field agent."

Rayne pointed to the girls' names as she called them out. "Aria Moore, Elianna Martin, and Zoey Garcia are competitive cheerleaders."

At the look on his face, Dex obviously didn't understand the sport.

"They're not the raw-raw pom-pom cheerleaders. These girls can do a back tuck from a standing position and land on their feet every time. It's more like floor routine gymnastics."

He seemed to understand the comparison.

"All of these girls are excellent swimmers." She thought for a minute, trying to recall swim meets three years ago when she had first started guarding Robert Sedgwick. "Yes. They have all competed on the country club swim team for years. That's part of the reason they were on this trip. They wanted to swim the coral reef."

"Who else competes in the sport?" Dex glanced back and forth between the list and the school pictures that had been provided.

"They're all involved in at least two sports," she pointed out. "It's required by the school. They're quite physically fit. This isn't just any private school for girls. It's a STEM school."

Dex had that confused look on his face, again, so she explained, "STEM: science, technology, engineering, and mathematics. These girls are highly intelligent and very outgoing. That's the kind of young women that the school develops."

"You think they're smart enough to keep their mouths shut?" He shrugged. "We rescued some teenagers out of... where doesn't matter...but a couple of the boys and one girl had sassy mouths. Sometimes, I just wanted to smack them." Under his voice he added, "Ungrateful, overprivileged, little bastards."

Rayne heard every word. "These young ladies aren't like that. Given who their parents are, they're extremely politically aware. Many of them have stood in front of thousands of cheering, or jeering, adults, yet maintained their cool. Several first went on the campaign trail with their parents when they were toddlers. They learned the hard way that anything they say or do could appear online with derogatory comments before they were back in the car."

She tried a different approach. "Children of politicians are unlike your standard junior high school student. These kids have lived in the spotlight all their lives. They, better than anybody else, know what's expected of them in public. They are much more emotionally in control than most kids their age."

Dex nodded. "So, what you're telling me is that I'm not going to have any prima donnas?"

"Just because they have manners and say yes sir or no sir, yes ma'am and no ma'am, and know which fork to use, doesn't make them little princesses who are afraid to get dirty." Rayne reconsidered for a moment, remembering Sophia's meltdown a few weeks ago. "But they do think like twelve-year-olds. Now, that's not to say they aren't going to have a total breakdown once they know they're safe."

Dex nodded. "That happens with adults, men *and* women."

"Have you seen a lot of that?" The question had slipped before Rayne could hold it in. The feminine part of her wanted to know how many times he'd held female captives as they fell apart in his arms. Did he stop with consoling them? Had there been women on his teams? Did he end up in bed with them like he had with her?

He hesitated for a long time before he answered. "I've done dozens of rescues, and each one is different. I've had grown men break down bawling in my arms and I've had small children who never shed a tear but took my hand and their little legs kept up right beside me." He grimaced. "I've had women beat on me in a half-crazed state, thinking I was one of their captors and they were still fighting for their lives."

Rayne's heart bled for everything Dex had gone through. She reached across the small table and touched his arm. "You truly are a good man." As soon as she realized what she had done, she fought the urge to jerk her hand back. Instead, she gave him a little squeeze. Then as casually as she could, she returned her hand to her side of the table and folded them in front of her so as not to be tempted again.

"Unfortunately, the good guys don't always win." Changing the subject, he asked, "What do you know about the chaperones and the teacher?"

"Annemarie Rogers teaches science at the school. She's also their Girl Scout leader. The girls really like her." For the first time, Rayne tried to define why they admired her so much. "Ms. Rogers doesn't talk down to them. She treats them more like adults than children. She also listens to the girls. I think they may get more attention from her than they do from their parents." Realization hit her. "They spend more time with Ms. Rogers than they do with their parents."

"So, you think she'd be pretty levelheaded?" There was hope and admiration in his voice.

"Definitely. Her first concern is going to be the care and safety of the girls." Of that Rayne was sure. Ms. Rogers would keep her shit together in the current situation...unless someone tried to hurt one of them.

Dex nodded. "What about Lynda Thompson?"

"She was one of Mrs. Sedgwick's good friends." Rayne immediately caught herself. "The first Mrs. Sedgwick. She passed away two years ago of cancer. Mrs. Thompson often came around to visit Bette and she would take Callie to spend the night, or even the weekend. Other than that, I don't know her personally."

"Rita Garcia." Dex's pen rested on the woman's name on his list.

"I don't know much at all about her," Rayne admitted. "Zoey is a very nice, well-behaved young woman. Mrs. Garcia was always gracious when she came to pick up her daughter, but rarely lingered." She considered for a moment before adding, "I don't believe she cares at all for the new Mrs. Sedgwick. On more than one occasion I have seen her roll her eyes at something Angelique has said or done."

"Okay, let's talk about Angelique Sedgwick." Dex pierced her with his gaze.

Rayne took a deep breath and let it out slowly. "As

I'm sure you've read in her file, she is considerably younger than Robert."

"So, she's a trophy wife?" Dex offered.

"You might call her that." Rayne was proud of herself for that politically correct reply.

"Rayne, you are a trained observer. This is a critical situation. I value your opinion of this woman above anything in this file. Everything you tell us will help us." The tight lines around his eyes eased. "It's me, Rayne, don't hold back. Tell me your gut feelings."

He valued her opinion. She studied the man across the table for a long minute. "None of this ever gets written down. Nothing I say will ever appear in a file. I need to know I can trust you."

"I'm contracted to the Department of Homeland Security for this one mission." He grinned. "I don't write reports. I'm retired."

Rayne just threw the truth out there. "She's your worst nightmare as a hostage."

"Fuck." Dex dropped his head onto the back of the seat. "Tell me everything."

"To be honest, I don't know if she's that damn dumb or that good an actress." She tried to think of a good example. "She and Robert were at a party on Capitol Hill not too long ago when he took a senator aside to speak privately. One of the aides to an African ambassador approached her and said he'd love an introduction to her husband. The man knew that the congressman was on the House Committee on Science, Space, and Technology which threw up all kinds of flags for me. The idiot woman started rattling on about the location of the new bio facility, the deal still in negotiations for long-term space exploration, and the new computer program for the IRS."

Rayne shook her head. "I didn't know who to be angrier with, Congressman Sedgwick for telling these things to his wife, or Angelique for discussing national matters with a virtual stranger from an African nation. I think she wanted to appear to be well-informed and a confidant for her husband."

"Did you speak to the Congressman about it?" His face was hard to read.

"Of course." She was almost taken aback that Dex even had asked. She thought he knew her better than that. But they really didn't know each other at all any more. "And to his credit, Robert was upset."

"Good." Dex pressed on. "How do Angelique and Callie get along?"

"They coexist in the same house but rarely interact." Rayne told him the truth, the whole truth.

"Then why the hell did Angelique come on this trip?" Dex sounded incredulous.

"That's a very good question." Rayne sat back and folded her arms over her chest.

"Does she enjoy the outdoors? Hiking? Swimming?" He offered.

Rayne burst out laughing. "Angelique's idea of enjoying the out-of-doors is an open shopping mall where she's required to walk in the sunshine between stores. That can also be considered the extent of her hiking experience *if* she's wearing boots at the time. Ignore the fact that they are designer rather than rugged for mountain terrain. She does swim laps in the pool almost every day, but I doubt that she would get into the ocean. There are creatures in that water and one might touch her. Worse yet, fish poop's bad for highlighted hair."

He gave her a look as though Mrs. Sedgwick couldn't be that bad.

"Dex, I am not kidding you." She smiled sarcastically when she shared, "I overheard her tell her mother that she was going with friends on a private jet to the Caribbean to go shopping. Knowing Angelique, she'll work that in."

"How do you think she's reacted to being kidnapped?" Dex looked nervous.

Rayne had been edgy from the beginning. "She's probably falling apart like a toddler, or acting like a spoiled teenager. When Angelique and Callie are in the same room, the twelve-year-old is the adult. On more than one occasion, I've heard Callie chastise Angelique for her posts on social media. The woman doesn't have a filter. Thank God most people just ignore her, but all too often a journalist will corner her at a party and get her talking. By morning, Robert's Chief of Staff is on the phone as they discuss damage control."

"What you're telling me, is that Callie doesn't like her." Then he added, "but that's quite common for teenagers to hate the woman who replaced her mother."

"Of course," Rayne agreed. She was certain that was part of Callie's dislike of her stepmother, but it went beyond that.

"So Angelique Sedgwick is our problem child, would you agree?" Dex seemed to be summing up their discussion.

"Yes. Another reason why my presence is necessary at the breach. I've learned to handle the woman. I'll also be a liaison to the other women and girls since I know them personally." Rayne desperately wanted to be in on the rescue.

Dex considered her while she held her breath. "You

can be there," he conceded. "In the second wave with the medics."

Rayne would take that. She wanted to fly across the table and hug him, but she would never get that close to him again. He had burned her once—she wouldn't give him the opportunity to do it again.

Before she left, she wanted to know, "How is retirement going for you?"

He scoffed. "Before I got the call to head this mission, I was on Smith Mountain Lake fishing, enjoying the hell out of my retirement."

She looked at him, silver streaking his beard just as it would her black hair if it weren't for regular visits to the salon. "When did we get so old, Dex?"

"I'm not old," he retorted. "I'm only forty-four." He stared at her for a moment before he softly said, "and you're still stunning at forty-two."

She blushed. "You always knew how to make me feel pretty."

She stood, and like a gentleman, he did, too. "See, Rayne, we can have a civil conversation. All I ask is that you respect my position on this team. We worked well together before."

Rayne mentally added, *Up until* and wondered if those were his thoughts, too.

Out loud, she said, "We can do this. My goal is to bring home Callie, and the rest of the hostages to safety. I have to do this, not just for them, but for me."

She turned and walked back to her seat.

Why did he have to say she was stunning?

CHAPTER SIX

Stunning.

Really?

What the fuck was he thinking? In this day and age, a comment like that could be used against him as sexual harassment.

He chuckled to himself. There was nothing harassing about the sex they'd had years ago. Mind blowing? Oh, yes. Consensual? Absolutely.

And did he really care if she tried to bring him up on some kind of charges? Fuck no. Most senior officers who had been accused of inappropriate activity, much worse than calling a woman stunning, had been forced to retire. He was already retired and would be more than happy to return to that fishing hole on Smith Mountain Lake.

Besides, for a forty-two-year-old woman, Rayne looked great. Definitely physically fit, and certainly able to handle the strains of this mission.

Glancing at his hands, he couldn't resist opening her file...for the first time. He wasn't sure what, but something had kept him from looking into her life. His eyes immediately fell on her marital status. Divorced.

He wondered if his own file said divorced twice. He knew men who were on wife number four, or maybe five. Did their files simply say divorced? Men in the special operations field had a hard time keeping a wife—he'd known only a few over his twenty years' active duty to hold onto one woman. He briefly considered if it was the wife who was unique, or the husband who'd been able to balance the stresses of his job with the pressure of a family.

Knowing he shouldn't, he allowed himself five minutes to delve deeply into Rayne's past. Using computer programs exclusive to Guardian Security, it only took seconds to discover that she'd been married and divorced in less than a year. The husband had cheated. From the details, he never stopped seeing other women even through their six-month engagement, or after the wedding.

According to his FBI file—he had to be vetted because of her position and close proximity to the highest-ranking politicians in the United States—he was most likely a sex addict. Dex had to admit the man was good-looking in that sharp-featured, big-smile, hundred-dollar haircut, Disney hero way. Too bad he was a slime ball lobbyist who couldn't keep his dick in his pants.

No. The part that was too bad was that he'd talked his way into Rayne's head, her heart, and her bed. Dex felt bad for her that she'd been duped by this asshole. She deserved someone a lot better.

But, she hadn't found another man, yet. Her FBI files showed that she'd rarely dated since her divorce. She'd been squeaky clean at work and in her personal life, which had paid off with significant promotions.

The plane's nose tipped down. They would be landing soon. Dex probed into the bag of goodies provided by Homeland Security. He discovered several satellite phones, a decent set of team communication units, and a few other toys he'd examine in detail later. Grabbing the bag and heading to the back of the plane, Dex stood in the aisle and faced his team.

"We are going to be landing soon and we'll be separating on St. Thomas." He handed satellite phones to the women from the FBI, to Rayne, one to the DOJ men, and another to the two SEALS. He then distributed miniature headsets to his breaching team.

Facing the FBI women, he asked, "Is there anything you want me to run up the chain of command before I head to St. John Island?"

SSA Vanessa Overholt handed him a handwritten list. Smiling up at him, she added, "And don't forget about that raise."

Dex briefly scanned the list and couldn't see anything extraordinary. Many of these things he considered necessary and wondered why the FBI didn't automatically include them in a kidnap go-bag. He nodded and returned his gaze to the two women. "I'll see what I can do."

"We'd appreciate that," Vanessa replied.

"Did you have any problem getting additional counselors?" If anyone balked at the request, he would sic Si Branson on them. His old friend understood the powder keg this mission could become.

Vanessa smiled. "I got put straight through to the director

who promised me anything I needed." She pointed to the list he held in his hand. "Those are just a few things I'd like to get, if possible. If I requisitioned them through the system it could take months, but you mentioned outside resources."

Dex nodded toward the list. "I got this handled. Expect a call from Guardian Security. Their plane should be here later today."

When her eyes widened, they seemed to pop out from her tan face. "Can I volunteer, right now, to work with you again? I like the way you do business."

"Sorry, ma'am. As far as I'm concerned, this is a one and done," he admitted.

He looked to the six men then glanced at Rayne. "The eight of us will be jumping onto Seahawks and flying to St. John. We'll brief there."

At the pinched eyebrows and questioning looks from the special operators, Dex explained, "Rayne will be with us on the breach. She'll be on the second wave with the medics." Although none of them rolled their eyes, he could see the attitude. "Rayne and I kicked Boca Haram ass together in Nigeria. Don't underestimate this woman. Ever." With that warning, he returned to his seat.

After taking a picture of the FBI agents' list and texting it to Alex, Dex checked his secure email established for this mission. He was hoping somebody had good news. He smiled when the email from the USS *Abraham Lincoln* confirmed that his order of frog legs were already on St. John and had been thrown into the pot. His smile grew when he read that not two, but three Seahawks were sitting on the tarmac at St. Thomas airport.

The email from Si contained good news and bad news. The active-duty Navy SEALs were already working with the Virgin Island assistant police chief for St. John island checking every single residency.

On the flipside, they were having difficulty with the infrared on the satellites. Thanks to an Indian Summer heat wave, the late afternoon temperature was pushing one hundred and it was nearly impossible, even for cutting-edge technology, to differentiate between natural heat and body heat.

To top everything off, the tropical depression hundreds of miles out in the middle of the Atlantic Ocean had been upgraded to Tropical Storm Victor. They promised to keep an eye on it and update him if there was a change.

Ten minutes later, Dex leapt into one of the three Navy Seahawks and stepped ten years into his past. The culture shock hit him hard. Moving from the ultra-comfortable corporate jet with its plush leather reclining seats, subdued lighting, thick carpet and designer color scheme, to the ground-in dirt of the metal decking, and uncomfortable jump seats covered in frayed canvas, threw him back to his days as a lieutenant commanding a small team of SEALs.

Damn. He'd been happy back then. Living on the edge, filled with adrenaline, ready to take on the evil in the world, confident that the good guys would always win.

As the hydraulics groaned and the smell of jet fuel assaulted his nose and lungs, Dex wasn't sure if he felt old or energized. Maybe both. The crew chief handed him a scratched-up helmet. For what might be the first time ever, Dex glanced at the sweat-stained interior and wondered if it had ever been cleaned. When the hell had he become a puss? He mentally shrugged and jammed the bulletproof helmet onto his head and plugged it into the internal communications.

Rayne grabbed his shoulders as she was tossed into the helicopter by the crew chief. Heat from her palms raced through his body. He instantly grabbed her hips to help steady her.

"Sorry, ma'am, I was just trying to help you in," the crew chief yelled over the *whomp whomp* and whine of the rotors beginning to turn.

She laughed and her joy filled an empty void in Dex's heart.

"No problem. I'm sure you're accustomed to helping huge men in and out. I don't imagine you get many women on board unless you're rescuing them." Rayne quickly righted herself and put on the offered helmet. She had ignored falling into him, and he should too.

Her smile at the young sailor sent Dex an unwanted jab of jealousy. He had no business feeling possessive of Rayne. She had burned him in Nigeria by accusing him of purchasing hookers for the men on his SEAL team after they'd captured Boco Haram's hierarchy. Her accusations had nearly sent his career up in flames.

No. He needed to stay as far away from this woman as possible.

Dex sat in the outer seat staring at the beautiful turquoise water through the open door. He twisted so he couldn't even see her through his peripheral vision. He needed to focus on the mission, not the woman.

"How long will it take us to get to St. John?" Her voice came clearly through the headset.

"Only about five minutes airtime, once we get clearance from the tower, ma'am. Right now, we have several commercial jetliners stacked up." The pilot then reassured her, "Once we have our precious cargo on board, our flights will take precedence over anything else in the air."

"Thank you, lieutenant. I take it you're dropping us off at Cruz Bay?" She asked.

"Yes, ma'am. It's got the only helipad on the island, although we have scoped out several possible LZ's in case there are multiple injuries and we need to get closer." The pilots' comments touched on the biggest question Dex had concerning this operation. With so many hostages, they could almost guarantee that someone would be hurt, probably in need of immediate medical attention. He added the possible landing zones to his list of discussion points.

"We've been given permission to take off," the pilot announced. "Buckle up. You're going to get to see almost all of St. Thomas Island on the way. We'll be in Cruz Bay before you know it."

The minute they were in the air, Dex wanted to hang his head out the door and suck in the fresh air. He didn't care if he looked like a dog with his head out the truck window, cheeks flapping, his smile catching bugs. He loved that feeling as the anticipation of the mission built inside him. He almost missed fast roping down to the ground as the rotor wash pushed him into the earth. Nothing in the world felt quite like it.

The devastation of two, back-to-back category five hurricanes the previous year was still evident everywhere in the small town. Blue tarps covered at least twenty percent of the roofs. Some buildings were merely block walls standing vigil around nothing but air open to the scattered white clouds floating in the baby blue sky above. It looked as though most of the debris had been gathered and disposed, but a thirty-foot cabin cruiser remained wedged in a tree two blocks from the shoreline.

The pilot touched down on the baseball field as softly as a butterfly landing on one of the huge red hibiscus flowers hiding behind the chain-link fence.

Dex tore off his helmet and jumped to the manicured field. He jogged toward the blue-and-white lights flashing on a police SUV near the dugout.

"Dex Carson, Homeland Security." He held out his hand to a man the color of charred wood.

"John Winslow, Assistant Police Chief for St. John." After a brief shake, he crossed his arms over his chest. "Maybe you tell me what's happening on my island. I got a call from some director at Homeland Security before the sun was even awake. Then the National Park Ranger called me and demanded I get out to Cinnamon Bay. A bunch of little girls and their teacher were missing. My commissioner ordered us to start checking all the vacant houses. An hour ago, a bunch of Navy SEALs landed on this field. Some hotshot lieutenant told me they had been sent here to help, so I sent them with my men to check the houses. What the hell is going on? Nobody tells me nothing."

"Have you ever heard of Boco Haram?" At his question, he could tell that John had to think about it long and hard.

"You mean the terrorists in Africa? Niger? Nigeria? Or was it Chad?" John was homing in on the original location of the Islamic extremists.

"Actually, they wander throughout that whole area, but their leader, Aahil Mohammed Jaja, is somewhere on this island." Dex only hesitated a minute before he shared the confidential information. "He doesn't have just any ten young girls, their parents are senators and congressmen, including the daughter, and wife, of the Speaker of the House."

John swore in Caribbean creole.

"I think you may now understand the gravity of the situation. I know that your police commissioner has FBI training and that all of your police force has worked in human trafficking, so I don't need to stress that the first forty-eight hours of a kidnapping are the most important." Dex hoped his reiteration of the timeline would motivate the police chief even more.

"We need a place to meet, rooms for my team to rest, and access to food. Can you help me with that?" Dex pressed.

John waved his hand. "Already arranged. We are taking you to a private resort with exclusive villas. You will have privacy and all the comforts of home and no one will even know that you are here." He spoke into his shoulder radio. SUVs seem to emerge from every street surrounding them. "Everybody, get in."

When the helicopter crews didn't move, John yelled, "You come, too. Nobody going to touch." He looked at Dex, "My cousins will watch over the helicopters." The vehicles' drivers all stepped out and handed keys to the nearest person. Every local had at least one gun strapped to their body—most had several. "They all served in the military." Loudly he added, "They won't let anybody near these helicopters."

The locals nodded and formed a circle around the baseball field.

Their helicopter pilot jogged over. "Sir, I'd feel better if we left one of the crewmembers here and they rotated."

"Agreed," Dex ordered. An idea struck him. "John, how well do you know the homes on the island?"

"I know them all, very well. In 2017 we had to evacuate the island twice in fourteen days." The middle-aged policeman shook his head. "We were hit hard. It was the winds with Hurricane Irma that caused the most damage, then two weeks later Hurricane Maria tried to drown everything that was left. Since then I have carefully watched the island recover. So many gave up, and never came back." He cocked his eyebrow. "Why do you ask?"

"If I showed you a video, do you think you might be able to identify the house?" Hope stirred in Dex.

"Probably, but my wife, Mart, she'd know, for sure." His smile was proud and confident. "She's been selling real estate on this island for nearly twenty-five years. But let me take a look, first."

Dex glanced over his shoulder and saw Ethan walking by their helicopter. "Blade," he shouted. "Grab my bags, would you?"

The *thunk* at his feet drew Dex's attention.

"I brought them for you," Rayne said next to him.

That was so thoughtful of her. He knew they were heavy, but she didn't seem to have strained under the weight of both her bags and his.

She shrugged his backpack off one shoulder and handed it to him.

"Thanks." Dex quickly extracted his laptop and pulled up the video Jaja sent to the president nearly twelve hours ago. Before he hit the triangle to play, he warned, "I don't want you to concentrate on the message or the people. Look at the background. Help us identify the house." He then added, "This isn't easy to watch."

"I understand. We need to find these little girls and their chaperones." John nodded, giving the go.

Dex watched the policeman's reaction rather than the screen. He'd seen it enough. It still made him sick. John went pale under his charred-wood skin. The man was barely breathing. When the video ended, he took a deep breath and turned the color of red mahogany.

"Play it again," he said through clenched teeth. Glancing up at Dex he apologized, "I know you asked me to look at the background, but I couldn't take my eyes away from those scared little faces. I'll do my part, this time. Play it again, please."

A few seconds in, John demanded, "Stop." Without lifting his gaze from the small screen, he asked, "Can you back it up slowly?"

Dex did as asked.

Both men stared at the reflection in the mirror on the wall above the girls.

"I know that view," John pointed to the gorgeous scene that looked almost like an enlarged photograph that moved. Through a wall of windows, the turquoise blue of the Caribbean rippled as it pushed the tide toward the thin strip of white sand. Pointing to a tiny dot he proclaimed, "I'm pretty sure this is Trunk Cay, the small island that's part of Coral Reef Underwater Park Trail. Can you enlarge that?"

Dex tried to increase the size but it became very blurry and digitized.

John squinted as he continued through the video almost frame by frame. "I think this was taken from one of the homes off Centerline Road." He shook his head. "There has to be fifty houses in that area with almost that exact view." He looked up at Dex who held his gaze.

"We really need Mart. She'd know exactly which house."

"Call her," Dex ordered.

As the ranking police officer on St. John stepped away to make the personal phone call, hope rose in Dex. They might be able to wrap this mission up within hours.

Within a minute, John returned. "Mart is on the other side of the island but will meet us at the resort. We should both arrive at about the same time."

"Saddle up, boys. We're moving out," Dex shouted so he could be heard by everyone on his team and the helicopter crews. He glanced over at Rayne, who was already picking up her bags. "Sorry, I didn't mean to slight you by calling you one of the boys."

She glanced around, obviously satisfied that they were relatively alone before she said in a low tone, "You're well aware, I'm all female." She hoisted her large duffel onto her shoulder and gave him a salacious grin before she turned and walked away to one of the SUVs.

Damn. With just a look and the swing of her hips, she had him hardening.

CHAPTER SEVEN

As head of security for the Speaker of the House, Rayne
had been in some very nice places. But that was work.
She'd never had the opportunity to enjoy the amenities of
the resorts where they stayed. Even when she was off
duty, she was still in charge and had to set a good
example, so catching rays in her bikini on a beach was
never a good idea.

Maybe someday, she silently wished as she stood on
the deck of her private villa. She could step off the smooth
wooden planks into sugar white sand and walk a brief
hundred feet before her toes were in the warm crystal-
clear water of the Caribbean Sea. The colors spread
before her were a study in hues of blue. Where the water
fell off the coral edge, it was a perfect sapphire. As it
neared the shoreline, it blended to azure, lightening to
maya, then tinges of green turned it to tiffany before it
touched the shore as turquoise. The baby blue sky was
interrupted by clumps of dazzling white clouds that
gathered over the scattered forest green islands creating
the breathtaking territory of the U.S. Virgin Islands.

John had found them the perfect resort. Only a mile-and-a-half from Cruz Bay, the island's largest city, the upper-upscale resort entrance was nearly hidden between trees. In the lead car, their host had simply waved at the armed gate guard and driven straight to the beach, where they had taken three sets of villas in a row. As though he did this every day, John quickly assigned rooms and assured them they'd get keys at their initial meeting.

Rayne found her room between Dex's and the two former SEALs. The Department of Justice men had the room on the other side of their team leader. In the next building over, the three helicopter crews bunked. Farthest away was for the active-duty Navy SEALs who had arrived at the same time.

What a gorgeous place. It offered in-room spa treatments, twenty-four-hour room service from Cordon Bleu-trained executive chefs, and maid service anytime day or night.

Too bad their stay was tainted by the presence of the Boco Haram followers and their terrorist leader Aahil Mohammed Jaja.

Activity on both sides of her caught Rayne's attention. Everyone seemed to have taken a few moments for themselves to freshen up before taking in their temporary lodging.

Her phone buzzed with the text. *Mart is here.*

Time to throw herself back into work. With one last longing glance at Caneel Bay, Rayne headed toward the Congregating House, as it was indicated on the resort map, which had been turned into an on-island war room.

Standing next to John and talking with Dex, was a striking woman with flawless warm tawny skin. With her black hair pulled up in a large bun, her almond shaped eyes seemed to almost fill her face. Rayne was instantly jealous of her perfectly shaped eyebrows.

With Rayne's Asian facial features, no one could ever seem to shape hers correctly, not even the wonderful Vietnamese women at the salon where she got her nails done every other week. That was her one feminine vice. Okay, she had two; her nails, and her eyebrows.

Rayne tried not to stare but she was trying to determine if the woman's lipstick was primarily red or purple. It looked gorgeous with her skin and outlined the brightest white smile she had seen since a mission she'd been on in Hollywood. Her clothes were reminiscent of that op as well. The pencil skirt hugged her curvaceous hips and with the crisp white blouse tucked in, it perfectly accented her tiny waist.

This woman was drop dead gorgeous.

Rayne suddenly felt dowdy and underdressed in her comfortable camouflage utilities and jungle boots. After quickly washing her face moments ago, she hadn't bothered to even swipe on mascara. Lip gloss, on the other hand, was a necessity everywhere she went. Her lips always seemed dry.

Taking a deep breath, she decided she'd just have to get over comparing herself to the other woman. She was on a mission. In that heat and humidity, she would be wilting before she hiked two miles into the jungle. As Dex already pointed out, no one in that room would be looking at her as a woman. She was just one of the guys.

And the room was completely filled with large, very athletic men. Most of the active duty SEALs and helicopter crews were in their twenties with the exception of a few who were obviously senior noncommissioned officers. The men on Dex's team were mid- to late-thirties.

She suddenly felt like an old lady. She was old enough to have given birth to at least five of the young men in that room. If it weren't for Dex, she might be the oldest person there.

Brushing that frightening thought aside, she glanced around the room cataloguing every exit, every window that exposed them to a sniper bullet, and immediately eliminated every man in the room as a potential threat. She placed them all in the column as an asset. After so many years in the personal protection business, it was an automatic response.

Round tables were scattered throughout the room. Once again, the computer was hooked up to a large screen television on a side wall with the official shield of Homeland Security spinning slowly.

Dex glanced around as everyone took their seats. Rayne left a few empty chairs between herself and the small congregation at the front.

"Thank you, Mart, for coming so quickly." Dex tapped the computer and an image emerged. The only thing showing was the mirror on the wall, greatly enlarged. All those who'd been at the ballfield earlier knew that ten kidnapped girls leaned against the wall just below that mirror. Thank goodness that's all that showed. No one in that room wanted the real estate agent to see the entire video.

"This is a close-up of a mirror in a home on this island. We need to find this house. Do you recognize the view that it's reflecting?" As soon as Dex finished the question, the entire room went completely silent.

Rayne's heartbeat increased but she forced her breathing to remain slow and calm.

"This could be any number of homes on top of that

hill right behind us. There are several possibilities, but I can assure you it is located right off Centerline Road." She stepped back and swiftly grabbed the mouse, clicking before anyone could stop her. The video started to play from the beginning.

Dex jumped quickly and clicked to stop it. "Give me just a minute and I'll get you back to that point."

Frozen on the screen was an image of Jaja holding a gun to Mrs. Thompson's head.

Mart turned on him. "You will do no such thing. You will show this to me. You need my help, and I need to help that woman." She stretched out her arm and pointed at the screen.

Dex only hesitated a second before he clicked play.

By the time the video went black, silver tears streaked down Mart's pretty face. "I know this house." With the back of her hand, she wiped away the dampness. "I can show it to you. It's for sale."

"Ma'am, can you just give me an address? It's too dangerous for you to be anywhere near there," Dex warned.

Both Mart and John laughed. "This is a small island. Many of the streets don't even have names," the policeman explained.

Dex quickly grabbed the paper map and tossed it to Rayne. She unfolded it while he pulled the map up on the computer so everyone else could see. "Can you show me where it is?"

Mart drew a circle with a perfectly manicured fingernail around several streets running off the main road down the middle of the island. "It's in this area but it sits down into the woods. It's currently for sale for $2.4 million but the family is anxious to sell. I know I can get to a much better deal. The house is a bit dated. It was owned by that rockstar..." She turned to her husband as though for help. "You remember, the one who died about two years ago, he played the drums for that band—"

"Mart, sweetheart, it doesn't matter who owns it. I'm quite sure no one in this room is interested in purchasing it." John took his wife's hand in both of his. "They just need to find the right home, and hopefully those little girls." His voice broke on the last sentence.

"You know how I blabber when I'm nervous...and scared." She stepped into her husband's embrace and lowered her head to his shoulder as she wept quietly. Within a moment, she seemed to gather her emotions. Looking up, she marched to the map spread out on the table in front of Rayne. Bending over, she carefully pointed and mumbled, "Maybe this one. It's got a purple roof with weird angles."

Dex snapped his fingers. "I should've thought of this before." A few clicks later he asked, "Does this help?" He had pulled up the satellite view of the island and was quickly expanding the area that she had indicated.

"Oh, yes." Mart started naming off the owners of every single home in that area. "It's this one." She tapped on the computer screen as Dex used the mouse and circled it.

"Are you sure?" He pushed.

Mart lifted her head and looked as though she had just been insulted. "Of course I am. I know every home on this island. You will need to come down this road and pass this first house. This map is terrible. There is a road that continues all the way to this house. It's a paved road. When the place was built, they didn't want any neighbors so they purchased everything surrounding them that wasn't part of the national park."

A quick glance around the room told Rayne what she needed. Every man on the breaching team was already assessing the ground for infiltration and evacuation. She had already made her mental evaluation.

Dex enlarged the indicated house. "You're positive it's this one?"

"Most definitely. I've shown that house multiple times, I just haven't found the right buyer for it yet. I encouraged his children not to take the furniture, but they listen to me? No. I even offered to help stage the home with furniture from this wonderful place I know in St. Croix, but would they do that? No. They want to sell the home as is." Mart shook her head.

Obviously, what was going on inside that home suddenly hit her. With shaking shoulders, she stared at Dex. "Get that horrible man out of that house and off my island." She stepped to Dex and grabbed his hand. "If...*when*...when you rescue those women, and all those children, afterward, you come back here and visit St. John. This is a beautiful island, and he has made it filthy by his presence..." She sniffed. "I will personally find you the nicest place on this island to stay, and you stay free, for as long as you want." Shaking her head, she pleaded, "Get him before he hurts those girls."

Dex awkwardly patted her back. "Thank you, Mart. We really appreciate your help. We can now go after them." He turned her toward her husband and with an unspoken exchange, John took her from the room.

As soon as the door clicked behind Mart and John, Dex announced, "Let's get these fuckers tonight."

Twenty minutes later, after a heated debate about

exactly what time would be optimal for the raid, John stepped back into the room. "Secure everything," the local policemen yelled.

Max immediately flipped over, computers were closed, and the screen on the wall went blank.

"What the fuck, John?" Dex growled as he strode toward the newcomer in the room.

"Not a word until I say," John warned then stepped back out the door and gestured for the resort staff to enter.

Rayne wanted to smile as the highly trained staff looked straight ahead, quickly set up a buffet table, then marched single file out the way they'd come in.

When the last person left, John closed the door and didn't speak for nearly thirty seconds. "I don't know what time you last ate, but I know what you're preparing to do tonight, and you'll need to fuel your bodies. Although the resort staff's trained to keep their mouths shut, this is a small island. Word travels fast." He gestured to the heavily laden tables. "I guarantee the food is excellent. Please eat."

No one certainly had to invite the active duty sailors more than once, but they all looked to Dex for approval. It took a lot of high-octane food to keep them going. Especially when it smelled that delicious.

"Food is an excellent idea, John. Thank you very much." In a louder voice, he added, "You can eat and think at the same time."

Rayne waited until all the men had gone through the line before she turned to Dex. "Everyone has eaten, and a few of those SEALs over there are still looking hungry and forward to seconds. But they're well aware that their leader hasn't been served yet. Let's grab a plate while there still some left."

His smile touched her heart. "You're looking after me like a good executive officer." He glanced around the room. "I think you're right. It might be a long night and you'll be thankful for the carbs you're eating now."

Bantering like they did years ago, she patted her hips, "I'm never thankful for carbs. They have a tendency to settle in all the wrong places. The older I get, I swear the farther gravity is pulling everything down."

They stepped at the end of the line and she handed him a plate.

"Looks to me like everything is still in the right place," he said in a low tone next to her ear, quiet enough so only she could hear. Glancing over her shoulder, she watched his smile grow. "When this mission is over, I'll be more than happy to check."

Everything in her body went cold. The last time they were together after a mission didn't turn out well for her. She had nearly lost her job because he had not corroborated her alibi. He'd lied. They'd spent the night together and he'd been too embarrassed to tell the investigators that he had been with her.

Rayne was a smart woman. Burn me once, shame on you. Burn me twice, shame on me. She would never sleep with someone she even remotely worked with, so there was no way in hell she'd find herself naked with Dex Carson again.

But she *had* flirted with him, and that was on her.

When only she and Dex were left in line, she straightened her back and squared her shoulders, her full plate a shield between them. "I'm sorry Comman—" She corrected herself, "—Dex, I spoke inappropriately. I promise to keep my comments completely professional from here on out. Neither of us needs distractions."

"Rayne, we have a past and you can't change history." He held her gaze until she looked away, pretending to search for a seat. "I misspoke as well. If you decide to bring me up on sexual harassment charges, please wait until after we've rescued these hostages. They're more important than your hurt feelings right now." Dex skipped the rest of the table and took his plate to where their breaching team sat together.

There was only one empty chair and Rayne was sure he'd take it. She couldn't stand to see him shut her out, again, so she added a few more things to her plate before she turned to find a seat. To her shock, he pulled up another chair to the table and all the men had shifted, leaving the empty chair on the opposite side of the table for her.

Damn it all to hell. There he went, being nice again.

Hands filled with food and drink, she made her way to the table to join the rest of her team.

Three hours after darkness cloaked the island, Rayne stepped over a rotting log, thankful for the high-tech night vision goggles. This model was so much more advanced than the ones she'd used in Nicaragua. She was also amazed at the tiny communication system that embedded so deep in her ear it couldn't even be recognized unless someone was specifically looking for it. Somebody had claimed that Dex had secured the leading edge technology through his new job at some black ops company.

Glancing to her left and right, she could see her teammates as they slowly approached the house indicated by Mart. There were no lights on inside, even though they had checked the utility company and the electricity was still on.

The whole situation didn't feel quite right to her. Knowing Jaja as well as she did, because she had researched the man for years, he would never be inside a building without multiple guards layered around his location. Due to satellite problems, again, they had not been able to check for heat signatures inside or outside the house.

"Hold."

She froze midstep. Flipping her NVGs to infrared mode, she scanned the area, remembering to look up into the trees, which made an excellent sniper hide. Other than her team, there was nothing larger than a feral cat.

Earlier they had seen a herd of wild goats, a couple of sheep, and even a deer as they made their way from the road through the heavily wooded national park for the house. Many domesticated animals had been killed during the back-to-back hurricanes, or had starved to death when their owners had been evacuated. Those left on their own had created wild herds that were quickly becoming a problem, especially the pigs.

The night was black as thick clouds gathered overhead as a prelude to the approaching hurricane, blocking any light from stars or the moon. The perfect night for a raid, especially when it started to drizzle. Most guards didn't like to get wet so they would often move inside and take turns walking the perimeter. Even with Rayne's limited tracking skills, she could see that several boot-clad men had practically worn a path around the house and to certain lookout points.

But no one entered or exited while they had been watching for the past two hours as they slowly crept in. Only twenty feet from the basement door, they were on hold, waiting for Dex's command to enter.

Nope. This definitely didn't feel right. For the first time in many years, Rayne was thankful for her bulletproof vest, helmet, and additional weapons.

"On my count," Dex announced.

A river of sweat rolled down Rayne's spine and another between her breasts. It had been too long since she'd practiced breaching in full gear, but heat radiated up from the ground cooking the moisture falling from the sky. Humidity was a bitch.

"Going in on three."

She brought her semi-automatic rifle to her shoulder and continually scanned their six. Liam, the Navy SEAL from the State Department, would bust down the door and be followed in by Robert Taylor, the DOJ special forces guy.

As they cleared each section, Rayne and Will Edge, one of the DOJ medics, would move deeper into the house and then either assist in the fight or deal with the injured.

"One...two...three."

Ten minutes later, the eight members of the breaching team stood in the living room and stared at the very familiar mirror.

The house was empty.

CHAPTER EIGHT

They'd been moved and this was a much better place, Callie had immediately decided.

A few hours before, she had been in the bathroom when she'd overheard the conversation between Jaja and a man speaking some kind of weird dialect of English. She caught a few French words thrown in with weirdly accented English in an unusual cadence. She'd noticed that some of the locals had spoken the same way.

When the men first started talking, she'd quickly finished washing her hands and turned toward the door, but Ms. Rogers put her index finger to her lips and signaled for her to go back in. Obviously, their teacher wanted to hear the entire conversation as she leaned against the hall outside the bathroom door.

Turning on the water at the sink, Callie had sneaked back to the doorjamb, hiding, so she could hear too. The new man told Jaja that U.S. Navy helicopters had landed on the baseball fields and dropped off many men in uniform. They were all carrying guns and now helping the local police go door-to-door. Then they had brought more men back wearing all kinds of uniforms, with lots more guns. Now the helicopters were parked on the baseball field.

The man in the dark blue slacks and matching shirt wearing a baseball cap embroidered with Fix It Man had pointed to the other girls leaning against the wall in the living room. Callie didn't have any problem understanding the man with dreadlocks past his shoulders when he all but yelled, "You go now. I be helping."

Jaja immediately began to organize their departure.

When Ms. Rogers signaled, Callie left the bathroom. As she walked by the leader, he shoved her to one side. "You. Stand there. Don't move."

He turned his attention to Ms. Rogers. "Bring me Congressman John Martin's daughter."

Her teacher's eyes went wide before she agreed. "May Callie return to the group?"

Yes. Please. Please let me go back and be with my friends.

Although none of them had been hurt, yet, Callie knew this was a very dangerous man. She didn't like being singled out.

"No." Jaja just snapped. "She has to leave." His tone completely changed to one of anger and he raised his voice. "Bring me John Martin's daughter. Now."

Ms. Rogers quickly headed for Elianna, and the leader called out orders in that other language he used with the guards. The two men started yanking girls off the floor and shoving them toward her.

They brought Mrs. Thompson and Mrs. Garcia over to stand with her. Callie breathed a sigh of relief. At least if they were being separated there would be some adults with her group. She'd wait until they were alone before telling the others what she'd heard about the Navy helicopters and men with guns. It sounded as though there was a rescue in the works.

Thank God.

Although Callie had quit believing in the one and only, all knowing, superior deity, as she watched her mother die inch by inch from a cruel disease called cancer, she was willing to thank whoever, whatever, for sending help.

She wouldn't pray to him, though. She'd done more than her share of begging the unseen God that she had been taught since birth watched over them. Her prayers to make her mother better had gone unanswered. Her prayers to save her mother's life had been ignored.

Instead of loving her, taking care of her as her catechism instructors had promised, the omnipotent being had disregarded her pleas. Her father, too absorbed in his own grief, had thrown himself into his work and ignored her, too. Then, God the all-powerful being, had rewarded her for being such a good daughter during her mother's illness by sending her the Step Momster.

No. He would never receive another prayer from her.

Suddenly Callie remembered something her mother said the day she died. "I'll be watching over you from heaven, my sweet child." With frail hands, barely more than skin over bone, her mother had pulled Callie down to her and kissed her on the cheek. "I will always love you."

"I love you too, Mom." Their tears mixed as they'd cried, cheek to cheek.

Callie looked up toward the ceiling and mouthed, *Thank you, Mom. Help them find us fast.*

As the chosen girls were herded out the door, Callie

stood frozen in place. Her gaze scanned the girls and stopped when her eyes met Ms. Rogers. Her teacher mouthed, *It's okay. We'll be there soon.* Callie gave her teacher a small smile before her gaze fell on Angelique. Given all the problems that woman had caused, Callie wondered if they would bother to bring her stepmother with them. Part of her hoped that they wouldn't.

She was going to hell for that thought, for sure. She might not believe in God, but the devil, he was real. So was heaven and hell.

Jaja grabbed the new man's arm and asked in English. "You said your cousin was helping to guard the helicopters. Do you think he would disable them for us?"

The whites of the man's eyes grew huge. "No. Not him. Not any of the men there. They all served in the military. Most were in the Navy. They would beat me up for even asking. Besides, some of the pilots and crew have stayed with the helicopters. No one gets near them."

Jaja nodded. "Take these infidels and come back for the rest." He grabbed Elianna's chin. "I need you to talk to your father, and the President." He grinned. "Maybe, this one, we will show to the world."

Dreds, as Callie decided to call the new man, led the way to a white service truck with a logo matching the one on his hat. Acne Face and Grunt followed a few feet behind them, quickly lighting cigarettes the moment they were out of the house. Mrs. Garcia had her arm around Zoe right in front of Callie as they were marched to the truck that looked like a beat-up, rusting version of the brown UPS vans that delivered the packages of food to her house. The bumper was high, and she had to stretch getting in.

"No seats. You sit on the floor," Dreds ordered from the front of the truck.

Callie quickly found Mrs. Thompson and Charlotte sitting near Mrs. Garcia and Zoe. She planted herself next to them and crossed her legs, making room for everyone on this first load. Grunt and Acne Face seemed to have an argument just before Grunt stepped into the back with them and Acne Face closed the doors behind him. As the truck pulled out, the tools and equipment rattled and clinked, drowning out the noisy engine. With no interior lights, they were instantly dropped into the darkness.

Good. This was her chance. Callie grabbed the two adults and pulled them close, hoping they could hear her. "They are moving us because the Navy sent helicopters and lots of soldiers to rescue us." Callie glanced between the two mothers hoping they had clearly heard because she didn't want to have to keep repeating herself, afraid she might get caught by Grunt.

"Callie, where did you hear such a thing?" Mrs. Thompson's tone was cross, as though Callie had lied.

"When I was in the bathroom and the new guy showed up." At the confused faces she continued to explain. "Ms. Rogers wanted to keep listening, so she had me run the water. I sneaked to the doorway and listened too." She pointed toward the front of the truck. "He said that three helicopters landed twice with soldiers. The first bunch went house to house with the local police looking for us. When the second group came, they left the helicopters at the ball field."

"We passed a baseball complex on the way here. It's not that far away. Maybe a couple of miles." Mrs. Garcia sounded excited.

"Maybe they sent in some Navy SEALs," Mrs. Thompson added. "Carl has mentioned several times that if he ever got kidnapped, he'd want the Navy SEALs to rescue him because they are the best. He would know, too, since he's on the Senate Armed Forces committee. I'm sure he'd send them to save us."

The van slowed and took a very sharp left, knocking Callie into the mothers. Several girls bonked heads, but Brynn got slammed into one of the tool chests and a big wrench fell on her arm. She yelped in pain and started crying. The two older women quickly helped all the girls back to a sitting position.

Callie went to her best friend to try to calm her down while Mrs. Thompson took a look at her arm. "I don't think it's broken, but maybe when we get to this next house, we can get some ice on it."

The bumpy road was similar to the driveway of the house they just left. Callie was more concerned about her teacher than her stepmother, Cruella De Vil. "What are we going to do without Ms. Rogers?"

Mrs. Garcia threw her free arm around Callie. "Don't worry, Mrs. Thompson and I are with you. I'm pretty sure this guy is just going to go back and get the rest of our group." She glanced up at Grunt. "We won't let anything happen to any of you girls." With her promise, came a tight hug.

It was nice to have a mom hug her again, even though it wasn't her own mother. What was even nicer, was knowing that somebody cared about her.

As soon as the back doors opened, Mrs. Thompson immediately asked Dreds if there was ice. The handyman quickly ushered Brynn and Mrs. Thompson into the house. Callie tried to keep up but in the dim light of evening, she couldn't see where they had turned.

Stepping into a living room, she looked around, excited to find that this one had furniture. Her butt had started hurting in that other place. As soon as Grunt and Acne Face came into the room, they signaled for the girls to sit on the couches and chairs. Since there wasn't enough room, Zoe sat on her mom's lap in a big chair.

Callie could hear Mrs. Thompson and Dreds carrying on an intense conversation. A few minutes later, they emerged through a doorway onto the left.

"This house has food." Mrs. Thompson clarified, "And this wonderful man has agreed to allow me to cook for everyone. Don't get too excited, but I think I found enough pasta for everybody." She bent down and whispered something to Brynn who came over and sat beside Callie. Her friend had a bag of frozen corn resting on her forearm.

"Mum, you need to go." Dreds pointed toward the door. "The others are waiting."

"Would you explain to Mr. Jaja that you allowed me to cook food for everyone?" Mrs. Thompson stared at him. "I don't want to get in trouble for feeding the girls or the guards."

"No problem," Dreds reassured her. "You have to eat. We cannot starve you. You're a mum. Mums know how to cook. You have food readily back, yes?"

"I'll try, but it might take a while for the water to boil," Mrs. Thompson explained.

"You go cook. I go to the others." When Dreds smiled, he flashed a gold tooth. Callie thought only rap stars had gold teeth.

By the time Dreds returned with the other girls, Ms.

Rogers, and, darn it all, they'd brought the *b* with an *itch*, Mrs. Thompson announced the food was ready. She'd fried some vegetables and meat in butter which made a really decent sauce. As hungry as Callie was, though, anything would have tasted wonderful.

The food even seemed to make Mr. Jaja happy. He pointed to all the girls on the couch. "Go into the bedrooms and bring the mattresses into this room," he ordered. "Mrs. Thompson, take two girls and go clean the kitchen. Everything has to be put back exactly where you found it."

Callie dashed for Elianna, grabbing her hand and pulling her down the hallway. "Are you okay? You're really quiet. Did they make you say anything bad?" She hesitated. "Did they do anything bad to you to make you say what they wanted?"

"No." Elianna shook her head as she moved to the opposite side of the bed. "Nothing bad. I just didn't want to have to say those words."

The girls yanked and shoved until the queen size mattress was upended. "Did he tell the President what he wanted? Did he say what he wanted them to do so they would let us go?"

Callie got in front of the mattress and pulled while Eliana pushed from behind. "He wants a bunch of people let out of jail, not just in the United States, somewhere in Africa, too."

That didn't make any sense to Callie. The United States couldn't make some other country release prisoners. While the lookers were blocking the door, Callie quickly told her friend what she had overheard.

Elianna grabbed her in a hug. "We're going to get rescued."

"I hope so too." Callie whispered back.

With everyone working on it, the living room floor quickly became one huge bed. It had to be rearranged twice so Acne Face and Grunt could pace back and forth and keep an eye on them. Once Mr. Jaja was satisfied with the arrangement, he allowed each of the mothers to take the girls one at a time to use the three bathrooms in the house. They still weren't allowed to shower, but they were permitted to wash up a little using paper towels they found in the kitchen and a storage room.

Oh, what Callie wouldn't give for a shower. And a toothbrush. With any luck, they would be rescued soon.

When she and Mrs. Thompson returned from the bathroom in the master bedroom, Mr. Jaja ordered them to collect sheets and comforters from all the rooms. It took several trips under the close supervision of Grunt but by the time they brought the last pillows to the living room, the other girls had already made up the beds.

With a forced smile, Ms. Rogers announced, "This is like a big huge slumber party." She quickly added, "Without the pillow fights."

"But it's so early," Sophia complained.

"We can't turn on any lights and it'll be dark in just a few minutes," Mrs. Garcia explained. "We need you to be in bed now."

Even though it hadn't even turned dark outside, Mr. Jaja ordered, "Sleep. Now."

Callie didn't think she could sleep, especially not with the guards' boots *thunking* on the wooden floor as they paced back and forth. She crawled onto a king size mattress with Brynn on one side of her and Charlotte on the other.

Before she laid down, she glanced over into the corner

where Angelique remained tied and gagged. Luna had told Callie that her stepmother had created another scene while they were loaded into the van. Hopefully Mr. Jaja didn't know that she and Angelique were related by marriage.

"Good night girls," Mrs. Thompson whispered from the far side of Charlotte.

Callie scooched under the covers and rolled over onto her side. She'd try to sleep, but that seemed impossible.

CHAPTER NINE

"Fuck!" Dex wanted to shout but hissed quietly through clenched teeth as he paced down the beach.

The hostages had been there, and they'd missed them. *Damn it!*

He needed to move beyond anger and work the problem.

They had been in the correct house, that he was sure. Had someone warned them? Or was Jaja just being careful? It wasn't unusual for someone on the run to move from house to house, often in the middle of the night.

How are they able to move fourteen hostages without being seen? And where are they now? It was too fucking bad that the infrared on the satellites couldn't penetrate the thickening cloud cover.

Oh, yeah, that was another thing Dex had to worry about, Victor had been designated as a category one hurricane. Almost every anticipated path indicated that it would increase in strength and was headed close enough to the island to be affected.

What else could go wrong?

Dex slumped down onto the warm white sand, leaning against a thick palm tree, and stared blindly at the choppy sea. In his peripheral vision he saw something move. Instinctively, he grabbed his gun.

Before pulling it up to his line of sight, he remembered that he was in the midst of a high-end resort. Although he hadn't seen anyone other than those associated with the mission, he was sure there had to be tourists staying there as well. Hidden in the shadows, still wearing dark camouflage, Dex sat quietly.

Noting the small body, slumped shoulders, and the way he dragged his feet, Dex didn't feel threatened in the least. He could overpower this guy with no problem. The person would take a few steps, kick the sand, sigh heavily, then drop their shoulders again and repeat the process. Obviously, the person was upset.

Well. Damn it. So was he. But his misery was not interested in company.

The person dropped to the sand about thirty feet away and rested his forearms on drawn-up knees.

Unhappy with the stranger's close proximity, Dex considered slipping into the small copse behind him and returning to his room. Both could have privacy then. But he had been there first and claimed that spot.

What a ridiculous thought. He needed to be solving the problem of how to find the hostages. As he started to come to his feet, thankful he was downwind of the intruder and the strong breeze coming off the ocean would carry away any noise he might make while escaping, he caught a whiff of something very feminine, fresh, and enticing.

Glancing toward the figure on the beach, their hands worked at the back of their neck. With a shake of the person's head, lengthy black hair lifted on a salt-laden gust as though it were reaching out to him. Long thin fingers combed through the strands after massaging her scalp.

Like an ethereal mermaid calling to him, Rayne sat alone on the beach. Dex had been connected to this woman in a way that he never had with any woman before or since her...not even with his wives. She had created a special place in his heart twelve years ago.

Then she'd smashed it all to hell.

His emotions swung from one end of the pendulum, loving her, to the absolute opposite end of hating this woman more than anyone else in the world. Mostly, she confused him. She had hurt him like no one else ever could, or would, again.

They'd worked endless hours together pouring over research, sorting through tips, trying to pin down the elusive terrorist leader, Aahil Mohammed Jaja. Sitting hidden together for hours, watching a house, a business, and even once a wandering caravan, they'd waited for the man who at that very moment was somewhere on that island with fourteen hostages.

It suddenly hit Dex that Rayne wanted this man more than he did. She would have taken tonight's failed attempt personally.

Decision made, he closed the distance. "We'll find them," he tried to reassure her.

In a blur of long black hair spinning through the air, Rayne was on one knee, her gun in firing position, pointed at his head.

"Whoa." Dex threw his hands up in the air. "Rayne, it's me. Don't shoot."

She released a long audible breath and lowered her gun. "You scared the shit out of me."

He grinned. "You need to go back and change your clothes?"

"Fuck you," she snapped and holstered her weapon.

There was just something so sexy about a woman with a gun who knew how to use it. The way she twisted her body to put her gun away emphasized her breasts even in the baggie utilities. With her last words echoing in his head, he missed their casual bantering.

He wasn't surprised at his growing erection. She'd always had that effect on him. In his mid-forties, though, he wasn't sure if he should be proud that he could be ready so fast or be disgusted with himself that he couldn't control his dick.

"So, you want to fuck me?" He gave her what he thought of as his panty-dropping smile. "If that's what you want, I could be convinced."

She shook her head. "You'll never change, will you?"

Enjoying this nonwork conversation more than he thought he would, he kept poking the bear. "Oh, I've changed, in many ways." Obviously, though, not where she was concerned. His body still wanted her. Or maybe it just needed to get laid in a post-adrenaline testosterone spike. "I've gotten better with age. I'll be happy to give you a demonstration of the improvements."

He moved in closer. He'd liked to pull her to him, tease her with kisses running down her neck, then continuing as he stripped her out of camouflage, exposing that soft skin, nipping and nibbling. When he reached her core, he would gently separate her wet folds and suck on her clit until she screamed his name. Exactly like he had twelve years ago. The one and only time they had shared their bodies.

"I take that back, you have changed." She gracefully came to her feet. "You seem more relaxed. You used to be constantly...tense...hyperaware to the point of it almost being a nervous tick. I think retirement has calmed you."

He chuckled. That certainly wasn't the line of thought where he was headed, but he could change conversational directions. He had no business thinking about sex with this woman anyway. Picking up on the flow, he noted, "I've been on more missions since I retired than I did in the last five years in the Navy. As commanding officer of over a hundred SEALs, I swear all I did was sign papers and go to meetings."

"That's what I love about my job, most of the time I'm actively on duty," she explained. "As head of the Speaker's detail, I have to make a schedule and a few other personnel kinds of things, but mostly I guard Congressman Sedgwick."

"That's good that you like your job. I got to the point where I hated mine," Dex admitted.

"Why? What happened to the forever and ever career man?" Rayne glanced longingly down the beach. "Do you mind if we walk?"

He started to walk away from the well-lit villas. "Sure. I need to stretch my legs."

In amiable silence, they walked side-by-side, not close enough that their arms accidentally touched. The wind seemed to blow harder with every step as the sound of the waves rushing to shore increased in volume.

"You never answered my question," Rayne pinned him.

"What question?" He volleyed back as though he'd forgotten.

"What changed your mind about a thirty-year career?"

He let out a long breath as he considered his answer. "Politics...on every level imaginable."

She walked closer to him. "Did you say politics? Your voice got lost in the wind."

"Yeah. Politics. They are everywhere at that level." He shrugged. "By the time you're looking at getting promoted to captain, the ring knocker club pulls in a tight net."

"Ring knocker club? What the hell is that?" She stepped a little closer to him and tried to match his stride in the shifting sand.

"I didn't go to the Naval Academy, nor did I belong to any national fraternity." He didn't want her to get the opinion that he gave up on the dream, just that the dream changed, as did he. "The higher rank you get promoted, the more the selection board looks at everything you've ever done. I never commanded a ship. I was never in charge of multimillion-dollar airplanes. The SEALs run a lean team compared to an air squadron or as the captain of a small ship. Usually, the higher the rank the more people you command and the more costly the equipment."

His smile was wry when he continued, "I had only ever been responsible for just over one hundred men as a commander. Compared to a fighter jet, rifles and bullets are cheap." He shrugged. "All I ever wanted to do was be a SEAL. I was lucky, though. For twenty years I got to be a SEAL. Very few sailors can ever say that. Many are only in that specialty for one or two tours."

Another gust of wind passed over them.

"Then I got to retire. I'm only forty-four years old, and the government pays me for breathing." He thought about some of the other benefits of military retirement. "And I have damn good health coverage."

They came to a chain-link fence with concertina wire on top. Dex thought that might be a little overkill, but it wouldn't stop any of his men, so perhaps it was necessary. Wordlessly, they turned and headed back.

"So, now that you retired," she giggled, "or *will* be retired when you finish this mission, what are you going to do with your life? What's on your bucket list?"

Fuck. Dex had never thought about his bucket list. "I want to fish. A lot." He smiled over at Rayne. "You like to fish? I have a boat. I can take you fishing." For the first time since he left Smith Mountain Lake and boarded the helicopter for D.C., he wondered where *Reel Peace* had been taken. He was sure that Si had it put in a safe place.

Her broad smile touched his heart. "You want to take me fishing?" She laughed. "The Dex Carson I knew might ask me to join him at the shooting range, but fishing? Is that what you did for entertainment with your wives?"

"Fuck. No. They didn't want to go." Back then, he used fishing as a way to escape the house, and his wife. During both marriages. He couldn't remember asking them if they wanted to go along. He'd just pack up early in the morning and head out for the nearest stream or lake. No. Neither of his wives was ever interested in a day on a lake drowning bait.

Glancing over at Rayne, though, he could see her sitting in his bass boat. She was adventurous, unlike his exes.

"So, it's a date. When we get back home, we'll go fishing." It was a statement, not a question.

"I'm going to be the one to cook the fish," Rayne insisted. "Unless you've taken cooking classes."

Dex was a little insulted. "I can throw some butter in a pan and put a filet in there or cook it on the grill. I've even learned how to microwave potatoes."

Her light laugh touched the part of him that had been empty for a long time. "Like I said, I'm going to cook them. I'll let you chop off the head and peel off the skin though. Just the thought of that grosses me out." She shivered dramatically.

"Deal." He stopped and held out his hand so they could shake on it. When she slid her soft palm against his, he was tempted to pull her to him and seal the deal with a kiss. Instead, he shook it once and let her go.

"Besides fishing, what else is on your bucket list?" She asked.

"Oh, no. Your turn. What's on your list?" He wasn't going to move until she told him at least one thing she wanted to do in her lifetime.

Rayne stared out at the turbulent sea. "I want to go to a place like this when I'm not working." Her smile didn't reach her eyes. "When I was first assigned to Congressman Sedgwick, his wife, Bette, had just been told her cancer was inoperable, and more chemotherapy wouldn't help."

She swallowed hard.

"I guess she liked the beach vacations on the Virginia shore, and he preferred to go to the Blue Ridge Mountains, so they compromised with one week in each location every year." Rolling her lips in, Rayne seemed to fight her emotions. Dex wanted to hold her in his arms, giving her the strength to go on. "Bette asked her husband to take her and Callie to a Caribbean island where they could be together as a family one last time." Her voice broke.

This was a tough subject for her.

She let out a long slow breath. "We weren't far from here. We stayed at the Waldorf Astoria Resort in Puerto Rico. A beautiful place. We took turns guarding the family, technically Congressman Sedgwick since he's the only one who qualifies for Secret Service protection. It was easy duty. His office had arranged for an exclusive villa for the family, and there was one for us next door. The view was magnificent, but I couldn't enjoy my downtime lounging on the beach or having a mojito. That would've been totally inappropriate."

The thought of Rayne in nothing but a string bikini laying on the sand at their feet painted an image in his mind he hoped never would go away until it could be replaced by the real thing.

"That will only take a couple weeks. What are you going to do after you get tired of looking at sunsets and your body has turned golden brown?" He hoped to refocus her mind on happier bucket list items. "What's next on the list?"

She giggled. "You're going to think this one is silly...or possibly a bit strange."

Dex mentally prepared himself for anything she could possibly say. "Hit me with it."

"I'd like to see an X-rated movie," Rayne confessed. "I've never seen one. To be honest, I've never been brave enough to walk in by myself to watch a movie like that."

It took everything in him to hold back his laughter. She was blushing. The woman he'd watched bust through a door and kill three Boco Haram terrorists, was fucking blushing.

"Uhm, isn't that something women do together? Like in a big group?" As though the idea had just struck him, he blurted, "You know that you can get X-rated movies on television, right?"

"Yeah, but that's like watching porn," she retorted. "I'm talking about the movie theater affect. Seeing... everything on the big screen."

"You watch porn?" He asked the question before he thought better of it.

"Don't you?" She volleyed back as though they were discussing bacon and eggs for breakfast.

He wasn't going to admit to his viewing preferences.

Giving it only a quick thought, he hadn't watched pornography in years. His television viewing was limited to Jeopardy while eating supper, then he flipped over to the National Geographic or Smithsonian channels while his food settled. Within an hour, he had a book open. He was currently on a kick of reading about the early Presidents.

He needed to change the subject, and fast. "Name something else on this list of yours. How about skydiving?"

"I've already done that. It was fun, but I don't think I need to do it again. It's your turn," she encouraged. "Tell me something that you want to do before you get too old."

Dex had to think about it. As a Navy SEAL, he had jumped out of an airplane at 30,000 feet and dived a hundred feet down into the ocean. He'd gotten to do so many fucking fantastic things in his life. There had to be some challenges left. "I used to want to raft the Colorado River through the Grand Canyon and camp along the way. I've slept in the dirt enough in my life, so, maybe I'll just go see the Grand Canyon and stay in a nice hotel with room service."

Rayne nodded in agreement. "I've never seen the Grand Canyon, either." She smiled over at him. "Thanks. That's going on my list. And I'm with you on the hotel with room service."

A gust of wind picked up loose sand and tossed it at their ankles. Lightning leapt between clouds on the horizon. Dex could see the resort lights about a quarter mile away. They should easily make it back before it started to rain. "Next item on that bucket list of yours."

"You're going to think this one is ridiculous because I could do it any time, but I'd like to see every display at the Smithsonian." She slowly shook her head. "I spend most of my day less than two blocks away, yet I've never taken an hour to walk through the National Museum of Natural History." She reached out and touched his arm. "Did you know that the Hope Diamond is there? It's like the United States has its own crown jewels."

Heat radiated up his arm. With the next beat of his heart, it was as though she were in his veins, spreading throughout his body. He liked it. There was something so right about that feeling of Rayne being part of him. He couldn't stop his smile as he looked at her. "So, you want to go see all the fancy gems?"

She squeezed his arm slightly and she infused him with her excitement. "Yes, but I want to see everything they have, from prehistoric animal fossils to the dresses of the first ladies."

When she started to lift her hand off his arm, he grabbed it and intertwined his fingers through hers. Half expecting she would jerk away, he was extremely pleased when she held on tight. "Most people have trips to exotic places on their list. Do you?"

"Of course, but that's under a different category," she proclaimed. "I want to go to New Zealand, when it's wintertime in D.C., and I'd like to buy a handcrafted Maori bone."

Dex had no idea what the significance of that would be, but if that's what Rayne wanted to do, she was welcome to it. The idea of going somewhere warm in the midst of a freezing cold D.C. winter sounded like a great idea, though. Inwardly he smiled. He could go there, now that he was retired. Nothing was forcing him to suffer through sleet, slippery roads, and overcast skies. Maybe he'd go someplace warm for the winter.

"What are some of these other categories that are part of your list?" He might have to start a list of his own.

"I have a few adventurous things that I'd like to do, a couple things dealing with nature and wildlife, I have a category for entertainment, one for food." She shrugged. "And some things that just don't belong in any one category."

They approached the end of the shadows cast by the trees and Dex came to a stop. Light spilled from the villas beyond, but he wasn't ready to let go of Rayne. There, in the darkness, it felt as though it was just the two of them. The moment they stepped into the light, they would return to the reality of terrorists and hostages. He wanted to hold on to the peace he had found with her for just one more moment.

"When we get back, we're going fishing." With his free hand he ran his fingers through her hair next to her temple. Slowly, giving her time to pull away, he lowered his head and brushed his lips over hers.

With the wind at her back, her long hair enveloped him. It was as though part of her was wrapping around him, binding them together.

Rayne let go of his hand and lifted both of hers to his face. She pulled him down and took over the kiss. Her lips were demanding, seeking more.

He pulled her body tight to his just as the clouds opened and poured buckets of water over them. He ignored the fact they were getting drenched and concentrated on the feel of her lips on his, their tongues tangling in a dance as old as time.

Both of them were breathing hard as they separated at the same time. Dex dropped his forehead to hers.

She tilted her head slightly and gave him a quick kiss. "Thank you."

"What? Why—" He didn't understand, or perhaps he hadn't heard her correctly over the smack of rain hitting the leaves on the trees behind them.

Her smile was warm and sincere. "Kissing in the rain was on my bucket list. I had just never imagined it would be you."

Water droplets fell over her face as she turned it up toward the sky, her eyes closed. She had never looked more beautiful. He dropped his lips to hers, tenderly kissing her one more time.

There was nothing better than Rayne in the rain.

His satellite phone rang and they both jumped apart as though they were teens caught necking.

With nothing more than a glance toward the lights, they both sprinted to their villas.

CHAPTER TEN

Rayne peeled off her soaked clothes as she headed straight for the shower. Dex had heated her from the inside out, but the second she stepped into the air-conditioned villa, a cold bucket of reality dumped over her.

What the hell was she doing kissing Dex Carson?

She had wanted to get away for a few moments to clear her head. 'Disappointed' couldn't begin to describe how she felt. She'd walked room to room in the empty house. The girls had been there. The house still held the scent of teenage sweat, hints of stale cigarette, and men in need of a shower, but it was the discarded feminine products in the hall bathroom that confirmed their presence in her mind.

She'd sauntered down the beach needing to cleanse away the anger of being so close yet missing them. She was livid with herself for not thinking like an investigative agent. Rayne knew that Jaja would move, and often. His backup plans had backup plans. She needed to cast off the emotions in order to concentrate on finding the girls.

Stepping under the warm spray, she savored the feel

of water pelting her skin. She grabbed her shower poof and squirted her favorite gel, then squeezed it into a lather. As she soaped her body, the light exfoliator stimulated her already aroused nipples into hard pebbles.

Where was a man when she needed one?

Right next door.

One who knew exactly what to do with her body. Given the size of his erection as he had kissed her, he was willing and would certainly be able to satisfy her.

Damn Dex. Just being around him had stirred emotions that she had kicked into a dark corner twelve years ago. Back then, she had wanted him, needed him, more than she'd ever needed any other man. She had even dared to think long term with him.

She was such an idiot, then and now. He had kissed her, but could she let it go at that? No! She had to take control and kiss him back. As though it was a sign from God, it started to rain. She'd been elated. So, what did she do? She kissed him harder.

Kissing in the rain had been on her list since she was a little girl dreaming of her knight in shining armor coming to rescue her from a house filled with children.

Smack in the middle of seven kids, she'd always felt like the forgotten one. She'd excelled at sports, hoping to be noticed, but there was constantly an event at church or activity in the community where her parents were expected to attend. They'd missed almost all her games. When not at practice, she hid in the bedroom she shared with her two older sisters and studied, or read romances, dreaming of that hero who would pay attention to her, listen to her and think that she was brilliant, then whisk her away where it was only the two of them.

Sometime in high school, Rayne realized that the

armor worn by most knights wasn't shiny after all and that no one was coming to save her. She could don the bullet-proof armor and save herself. She could also rescue others. The champion didn't always have to be a man.

She also liked being feminine. She thoroughly enjoyed getting dressed up and going out on a date, especially if the man proved interesting. She'd had a few one-night stands—her choice, not his. Rayne had learned early on in the dating game that men were rather clueless when it came to sex. They often needed instruction, and she was willing to add to their education if it resulted in multiple orgasms for her.

On the rare occasion, she'd find a man who interested her over dinner as well as in bed. Dex had been like that. She'd enjoyed his intelligence from the first day they'd met. Although they'd never even kissed until after the successful mission in Nigeria, she'd somehow known he wouldn't need a map to find her clitoris.

She was right. For hours he had taken her to heights beyond reach with any other man. Then his phone had buzzed. He'd crawled out of her hotel room bed without a word, a kiss, or a backward glance.

Rayne hadn't seen or heard from Dex until twelve hours ago.

His kiss had taken her back to that hotel room with sex-dampened sheets. Her brain had filled with a lusty need for more of this man's body and what he could do to her...for her...with her.

Why did being with him feel so damn good? Why did their conversation have to be so easy? Why did she want him so fucking bad?

Her shower held no answers.

Finally warm once again, she turned off the water and stepped out. Someone was beating on her door.

Quickly wrapping a towel around her naked body, she trotted to the door and looked through the peep hole. Dex stood on her porch with wet hair and clean dry clothes. "Rayne, open the door. We have new intel. We have to go. Now!"

Without remembering that she wore nothing but a towel, Rayne opened the door. "What's going on?"

Dex's gaze fell down her body. He stared at her bare feet with red painted toenails before his eyes slowly crawled upward. The bath sheet hung below her knees and was tightly wrapped across her chest, completely covering her small breasts. There was certainly nothing sexy as far as she was concerned.

"Dex?" She asked impatiently.

His eyes met hers. "Uhm...since you're..." His eyes scanned her body once again. "Looks like you just got out of the shower. Dress as quick as you can and meet us in the war room."

"What's going on?" She asked for the second time.

"Video." He seemed to have difficulty getting the one word out. "Jaja sent another video to the President. Conference call in five minutes."

"I'll be there." She practically slammed the door in his face and dropped the towel on the way to her duffel bag. She was used to getting dressed in a hurry. She threw on a tank top, stepped into camouflage cargo pants, and grabbed her boots, throwing clean socks inside them. Rushing by the bathroom, she scooped up her brush with hair ties wound around the handle. Within two minutes she was sprinting down the sand. Thankfully, the band of rain had passed over the island. The nearly full moon lit the way while the black sky was filled with stars. She wished she'd been able to take a few minutes to absorb the beauty of the night.

Quietly sliding into the back of the darkened room, she leaned against a wall just as the Department of Homeland Security logo stopped spinning and Silas Branson appeared on the large flat screen.

"Eleven minutes ago, the President received another video from Aahil Mohammed Jaja. Dex, you'll have to retrieve it from the secure file." Silas slowly shook his head. "He used one of the kids this time. She was identified as Elianna Martin."

Rayne's heart leapt. She was thankful and sorry the same time. Part of her was grateful that Jaja hadn't chosen Callie, while she felt terrible for Elianna's parents.

"Her father is Congressman John Martin, the chairman of the House Foreign Affairs Committee. Jaja made her hold up a list of names of men he wants released from U.S. custody, three from Nicaragua and two from Chad. He made it clear that he wants the President to put pressure on these countries to release his men."

"The President has no intention of doing any of that, right?" Dex asked.

"Fuck, no," Silas shot back. "We all know the policy, the United States does not negotiate with terrorists, even ones who kidnap little girls. Which brings me to my next point."

A weather map of the Caribbean filled half the screen.

Holy shit. That hurricane was big and headed straight for them.

"This outer band of storms has moved across St. John and cooled everything off, making it much easier to identify fourteen people most likely huddled together." He leaned his forearms on his desk. "We have analysts searching every inch of the island and data streaming in every second. We're going to find them, but we have a very short window of time before the next storm band crosses St. John. I want everybody to sleep until we've pinpointed the house. The strike is going to be fast and deadly. Be prepared to leave on a moment's notice. Everyone is dismissed except Dex's team."

Lights in the back half of the room came on. Chairs scraped across the tile floor as boots shuffled toward the exits. To Rayne, it seemed like there were a lot more people crammed into the small private room.

When everyone was gone except Dex and the six special operations men, she walked to the front of the room where the rest of her team was gathered around the table. "Who were all those men?"

"That's the complete team," Dex explained. "The platoon of active duty SEALs who were assisting local police all day, three helicopter crews, and us." He pressed a key on the computer and the screen came back to life. "The rest of them don't need to see this but I thought it might help us. I'll play it a couple times."

Rayne's stomach flipped as the camera zoomed in on Elianna's shaking body.

"Say hello to the President and tell him who you are." The female voice off camera sounded like Ms. Rogers.

"Hello, Mr. Presi—" Her small trembling voice could barely be heard.

"Speak up, child," demanded a male voice. "Shout if you have to."

She looked off to the right of the camera and her eyes held as though she were listening to someone important.

Nodding, she took in a jerky breath. "Hello, Mr. President. I'm Elianna Martin," she said in a louder and slightly less shaky voice. The girl's eyes kept darting to the right side as though for approval.

"Hold up the list so the camera can get a close-up," came the female voice again.

As the camera neared Elianna, her eyes became very big and she started to back up.

"No, Eliana," pleaded the female voice. "Stand still so he can get a good shot of all the names on that list. Hold it out in front of you toward the camera."

The small, dark-haired girl shoved the piece of paper in the direction of the camera.

"Try to hold it still, so the President can see all the names." Ms. Rogers was doing a good job of keeping the girl calm.

The camera moved back and Jaja was holding the gun to the little girl's head. "Mr. President, you have my list. For every one of my men set free, I'll give you back one of these pretty little girls. You have exactly twelve hours from the time I sent this video to let my men free before I start killing these hostages."

Jaja ran the muzzle of the gun down the little girl's jawline and leaned in very close to her ear. "You should hurry, Mr. President. I might have to give some of these virgins to my men before I kill them." His smile was cruel and didn't change his dead eyes. "After being fucked by each of my men, multiple times, in every hole in their nubile bodies, they will beg to die." The screen went blank.

Rayne's blood boiled. "I'm going to kill that fucker."

"Not if I get to him first," Dex pledged. "We're going

to watch it again, and this time keep an eye on the background, anything that would give us another clue.

On the second pass, they saw the corner of the now familiar mirror. The color of the walls matched the ones they had been in a few hours before.

By the fifth time they'd seen the same video, everyone agreed that Jaja had recorded this message before they had moved the hostages.

Rayne fought a yawn but caught Dex watching her.

"We need to sleep, too." Dex started gathering the map in closing down the computer. "I'll call you if anything changes. Like Si said, be ready to roll with moment's notice."

Without a backward glance at Dex, Rayne walked back to her villa, placed her nighttime camouflage gear in the exact order she needed to put it on, and crawled into bed wearing panties and a black tank top. It had been a while since she had practiced combat naps, sleeping deeply for a short period of time and waking completely refreshed, but it only took her a few deep breaths to fall asleep.

At 2:30 in the morning, approximately twenty-three hours after the girls were kidnapped, her phone rang. She awoke fully in an instant.

"Yoshida."

"War room. Now. We're going after them." Dex didn't bother saying hello or goodbye.

As Rayne walked into the war room, she was surprised that only her team was there gearing up. Some were strapping on Kevlar vests while others were Velcroing holsters to their thighs and ankles. Dex looked as though he hadn't left.

"So, what did I miss while I was sleeping?" Rayne dug

her custom-made bulletproof vest out of her bag and started to strap it on.

"About an hour ago, Si woke me up with the news that they had narrowed the possibilities down to three houses. We sent the active duty SEALs to check out each of the houses." He pointed to the map. "This was the only one that had guards patrolling the woods surrounding it. The others were all empty."

Rayne's heart began to beat stronger and faster. This was it. She had a good feeling about this one. It would be over before daybreak, hopefully. "What's the plan?"

"Dark and fast," Dex announced. "All the active duty SEALs are converging on this location and currently in a holding pattern. They are not to engage until we arrive."

She glanced around as she strapped her favorite pistol holster to her right thigh. "Helicopter crews getting ready?"

"We'll drive to this point and leave the SUVs here." Dex stopped lacing up his boots and pointed to a house about a mile from the target. "Once we've secured the house and the hostages, the active duty SEAL team is going to run through the woods," he traced a straight line between the two homes, "and bring the SUVs down the road to us. They'll then help us with the evacuation, escorting the hostages over to St. Thomas where they will turn them over to the FBI."

"With hours to spare before Jaja intends to start killing people," Ethan announced as he slid a nine-inch knife into a sheath at his waist.

Rayne wondered if he was going to be able to use that weapon and once again live up to his moniker of Blade.

"Ready?" Dex asked his team.

"Fuckin' A," Shep responded.

Robert Taylor and Devin Martindale, two of the Special Forces men from DOJ, gave him a thumbs-up.

Will, one of the medics, asked, "Is there any way Stephen and I can talk you into letting us go in with you?"

"No." Dex headed for the door. "You're going to have your hands so full within minutes you can thank me for making you wait." As he opened the door, he looked directly at Rayne. "You're with them."

"I know." She didn't like it, but completely understood why her team leader had made that decision.

Forty minutes later, she still didn't like being mandated to the second wave, but she was certainly thankful for the active duty SEALs who had silently taken out all the guards patrolling the perimeter.

The breaching team had moved up to the house while the SEALs had their backs, protecting the perimeter and assuring they hadn't missed any bad guys.

"On three." Dex started the countdown. "Counting. One."

Minutes ago, Dex announced that Si had sent an infrared picture of the house to his satellite phone. All the heat signatures seemed to be concentrated in one room on the backside of the house. They were too close together to get an exact count but it looked as though adults were mixed in with the children. On the live satellite feed at the Homeland Security Operations Center, they could see three people walking around inside the house.

"Two." Dex counted off.

Rayne, Stephen, and Will would go through the kitchen door at the side of the house once it was cleared.

"Three."

They opened the doors at the same time. Gunfire erupted immediately.

"One down," someone announced through their communications units over the squealing girls.

"Make that two," another voice came through Rayne's earpiece.

High-pitched screams assaulted her ears. She could hear the girls through the communications unit in her right ear as well as through her open left ear.

"Basement clear." That sounded like Devin, which would make sense since he was given the lowest level.

"I've got number three." Dex's voice was easy for her to identify.

He was safe. Relief rushed through Rayne.

"Rayne, medics, get in here and calm these girls down," Dex commanded.

With a nod, Will lead the way. The kitchen was empty but smelled of recently cooked food.

As Rayne stepped into the living room, she noticed eyes peeking from under blankets. A few of the girls sat upright screaming. The chaperones weren't sure what to do.

Rayne stuck her fingers into her mouth and whistled. The room fell into silence. "Young ladies, you all know me, I'm Senior Special Agent Yoshida. We are here to rescue you." She glanced at Dex. "Are we clear?"

Dex shook his head side to side.

"Girls," she ordered, "Chaperones, climb underneath all the mattresses and pillows. Don't come out until I come and get you."

"Upstairs clear." She was relatively sure that was Ethan reporting in.

"Do you see any more tangoes?" Dex was asking Silas on a separate communications channel.

When Rayne stepped back, she almost slipped in

blood. One glance at the headshot and her supper crawled up her throat. The girls couldn't see this. The kitchen was free of any bodies, so she'd send them there. It was also one of the safest places in the house, with solid wood cabinets filled with cans and heavy appliances.

After what seemed like the longest minute of her life, Dex finally gave her the "All clear."

She immediately started pulling girls from their hiding places. Lifting a couch cushion and tossing it aside, she found three girls. "Aria, Zoey, Elianna, you know me. I need you to do exactly as I say."

The girls nodded and looked around.

Rita Garcia stuck her head out from under a mattress.

Thank God. An adult. She didn't seem to be panicking. *Even better yet.*

"Mrs. Garcia, I want you to take the girls straight to the kitchen. Make them sit on the floor until I get there." With the slightest tilt of her head, Rayne indicated the dead body behind her. She watched the woman close her eyes and swallow hard. "I know this isn't easy, but I need you to move *now*."

Rita Garcia struggled for a moment to extricate herself from the mattress before she pasted on a smile. "We got rescued!" She extended her arms and herded the three girls in the direction Rayne pointed.

Next, Rayne found Luna, Sophia, and Gia and took them to the kitchen where she found Mrs. Garcia comforting the other three girls.

Once everyone was seated, Rayne explained, "In a few minutes, several Navy sailors are going to drive up in SUVs and take you down the hill to where there are three helicopters waiting."

SEAL IN A STORM | 121

"Callie was right," Elianna declared. "She said the Navy was coming for us in helicopters."

As all the girls began to speak at once, Rayne decided to return to the living room and get the last of the hostages. Before she left the kitchen though, she dragged Mrs. Garcia aside. "We have two medics with us. Do any of the girls need immediate medical attention?"

"Oh, I'm a terrible mother." She covered her mouth with her fingers. "I should've thought of that. We were in a different house before, and the ride was really bumpy in the van. Some of the girls got bounced around." She glanced down at the girls. "You see, we were in a different house."

Shock. Mrs. Garcia was possibly in shock.

"Mrs. Garcia. Rita. I need you to look at me and concentrate." When their eyes met, she continued, "Would you please find out if any of the girls need immediate medical attention? I'm going to send one of the medics in here to help you."

"Yes, yes, I can do that." Mrs. Garcia spun around and started with her daughter's friends. "Are you hurt?"

On her way back to the living room, Rayne called through her headset. "I need a medic to the kitchen. I'm pretty sure Mrs. Garcia is in shock. During transport from the previous house, a couple of the girls may have been hurt."

"Stephen here, I'm on it. Will is outside working on one of the active duty SEALs." He then added, "All the bad guys in here are dead. Good shooting, men."

Damn. An injury. Rayne hoped the young man wasn't hurt badly.

Returning to the living room, she started flipping over cushions and mattresses. She finally found Linda

Thompson holding her daughter, Charlotte. Cuddled close by, Ms. Rogers held Violet and Brynn.

As she brought them to the kitchen, she looked back into the living room, not seeing any more humps indicating the last two hostages, Callie and Angelique.

Don't panic. They're here. They're probably just flattened out so much you can't distinguish their hiding spot.

Ms. Rogers grabbed Rayne's arm as she was about to return to the living room. "I need a word with you in private." The teacher scanned the girls and chaperones before she pulled Rayne around the corner.

Both of them glanced toward the mattresses and pillows scattered around the room.

"They're not in there." Ms. Rogers explained, "About two hours ago, Mr. Jaja pulled Callie and Angelique down that hallway. We haven't seen them since."

Did Jaja hide them somewhere else in the house? Or did he take them away?

Rayne's heart sank. "Dex, we're missing two hostages."

CHAPTER ELEVEN

Fuck! Hostages were missing.

Not what any team leader ever wanted to hear in the middle of a rescue.

"I need everyone on the initial breach to search the house...again. Every closet, every dark corner, under beds. Rip this place apart." Dex had wanted to shout the order but held his emotions in check.

"Silas, check the—"

"We're already on it, Dex," his current boss affirmed. "Pulling live feed now."

The screech of tires and rumble of powerful vehicles turned his focus to the nine girls and three chaperones. "Rayne, I know your job is the Sedgewick family, but I want you to escort the women and children to the helicopters. They know and trust you. Help get them off the island."

Her nod and lack of argument surprised and pleased him.

When she grabbed his bicep, heat exuded from her

touch. "Keep me informed. Let me know where to meet you."

He leaned in close to the opposite ear from her comm unit and whispered as softly as he could. "Stay safe. We're not sure how many men Jaja has working with him on the island." He watched her beautiful backside as she strutted into the kitchen. He couldn't bear to think she might get hurt.

Dex shook his head to clear that horrible idea from his brain and focused on the hunt for Callie and Angelique Sedgewick. His mission wasn't over until all the hostages were safe.

After twenty minutes of searching, he flipped personnel to gain new eyes. Dex sent the active duty SEALs through the interior of the house and his breaching team to check the exterior. The rain had returned with vengeance, washing away any possibility of tracking them.

Stepping out onto the massive porch, he watched the three helicopters silhouetted against the gray dawn as the pilots took advantage of the lighter rain. In the morning haze, Dex scanned the houses nearby. Both teams had already searched every inch of the empty homes.

Where the fuck would that damn terrorist have taken them? Jaja had a two-hour head start. With a tired sigh, Dex knew they were back to square one. He dropped his chin to his chest.

He felt her presence before he heard her light footsteps.

"That was a deep sigh." Rayne rubbed her hand up and down his back. "In the famous words of Dex Carson, team leader extraordinaire, *we'll find them.*"

"I should be the one comforting you," he confessed as

he wrapped his arm around her and mirrored her movement.

"Yeah, but you're the one with the perfect rescue record. That's why I have faith we'll find Jaja and the Sedgewicks."

Her confidence in him bolstered his conviction. "Back to the War Room," he ordered. Dropping his hand from her back, he strode to the SUVs.

On their way down the hill, his secure cell phone rang. "Dex. This line is secure."

"Silas here. Sorry, Dex, but you're losing your SEAL team. They need to meet the choppers at the baseball fields and bug out. The admiral of the fleet off Venezuela is running away from the hurricane, which is now a category two with indications of intensifying. He wants his crews on his decks to assist with the aftermath if needed. Teleconference as soon as you're back in your secure room. Homeland out."

Fuck! Dex had mentally planned to use everyone available to him to start at one end of the island and check every house. That process would now take three times as long.

The SEAL behind the wheel took a short phone call as the first SUV in the caravan peeled off to the right. "Sir, I know you heard we're leaving. The other Jeep is headed back to the resort to collect our gear. We've been instructed to head straight to the ballfield."

"Thank you, lieutenant, for all your help." Dex wondered if he called the admiral himself if he could convince the man to allow at least a few SEALs to stay, but as a former SEAL commanding officer, he would've made the same decision. "We wouldn't have found these twelve as quickly without you."

Dex called SSA Vanessa Overholt to update her on the hurricane.

"We're already packing and taking this after-party to Quantico," she informed him. "The agency plane is prepping now, but I'm not leaving you."

"You should go back with everyone else," he insisted. "They'll be evacuating the islands soon."

"The other counselors can handle these hostages. I'm on your team which means if you're staying here, so am I."

He liked her tenacity, and deep down, he was thankful for her offer. He had no idea what condition the last two hostages would be in once they were rescued, especially after spending extended time with that monster, Jaja. There's no telling what he's doing to them, either physically or mentally. He didn't want to throw all of that at the seasoned counselor, so he kept it light. "You're just hanging around for that raise, aren't you?"

Her boisterous laugh lifted his heart. "If after this is over you want to give me a raise, I'm not going to argue. In the meantime, I'm going to do my job. You go do yours."

As soon as he hung up with his new favorite FBI agent, his Guardian Security phone rang.

"I heard you're in need of a new team." *Damn*. Alex had some high up connections.

"Yeah, you volunteering to come play in the mud with me?" Dex chuckled.

"Sure as hell beats the sand," Alex replied. "And before you ask, I talked with Silas's boss. We're sanctioned and getting paid to assist with your mission... since we were already here *vacationing* on St. Thomas."

"Fucking sneaky of you," Dex accused.

Alex laughed. "It's all about right time, right place. Besides, I would never leave one of my men hanging alone in the middle of a mission, and yours isn't over until those last two are found. Now, what can I do to help you?"

"We have a war room set up over here on St. John. Can you get the team here?" Without a helicopter maybe they could get there by boat. He gazed over the rough seas and knew any SEAL team worth its salt would tackle it, but Alex's mercenaries weren't all SEALs. Some were Army Special Forces and they even had a few Marine Recon and SpecOps guys.

"Are you still headed to the ball fields?" Alex asked.

"Pulling in, now." Dex looked across the chain-link fence to where the three Seahawks were landing.

"See your SEAL team off and hang tight. We'll be there shortly after they take off," Alex ordered. "Make sure all those civilians guards are gone."

Dex chuckled. "You don't trust anyone, do you?"

"Not unless they're on my payroll," Alex confirmed.

It only took a few minutes for the SEALs to load their equipment and bags. After personally thanking each one, Dex made the rounds of the civilians, requesting that they keep the SUVs until the other two hostages were found. Several volunteered to help with the hunt but Dex didn't want to be bothered dealing with civilians so he suggested they contact John, the police chief. That man had his hands full.

Dex gathered his team together and explained that more help was on the way and they should get out of the rain and wait in the vehicles.

Sitting behind the wheel made him antsy. He had always hated the sit-and-wait part of any mission. He felt as though he needed to be doing something more.

Dex yawned and stretched, fighting off fatigue. He

wondered if he could sneak in a twenty-minute combat nap. He laid his head back and closed his eyes.

Rayne drifted into his mind every time he tried to clear it. She sat in the next vehicle over carrying on an animated conversation with Will and Stephen. Having her so close during this mission brought back so many memories of their time together in Nigeria. They had become such good friends during those months prior to the failed op to capture Jaja.

Then there was their kiss on the beach filling him with warmth and desire for more. He wanted to touch those firm breasts of hers, take them in his mouth and suck hard, then kiss his way down her naked body. Finally, he would kiss her hard bud of desire before taking it in his mouth. In his dream, she tasted the same as she had over a decade ago. He could practically feel her scrape her nails over his scalp as she called out his name when she came.

"Dex."

Her voice sounded so real.

"Dex. You need to wake up."

He bolted upright and glanced at the passenger seat. Rayne was in his SUV.

When the hell did she crawl in? How the fuck did he miss her opening the door? Christ. He was completely losing his edge. Maybe it was a good thing he retired.

Concern written all over her face, she asked, "Dex, are you okay?"

With his big hand, he swiped the sleep from his face. "Yeah. Guess I fell asleep for a few minutes."

"We're all exhausted." She glanced down the line of vehicles. "Which is why I'm here. Do you know how many people are coming? Or how soon? Can some of the guys go back and get some sleep?"

They heard the loud *whomp whomp whomp* of a large helicopter in the distance.

"Sounds like the cavalry is arriving," Dex noted as he opened the door and got out of the vehicle. He couldn't stop smiling as an old Army Black Hawk headed straight for the ballfield. As soon as it landed, Alex was the first one out the side door.

"Damn, it's good to see you." Dex smacked his other boss on the back and pointed toward the vehicles. "There's space in each one. We'll pull out as soon as everyone is loaded."

"Which are we in?" Alex's question assured Dex that they were going to be riding together.

In just a few minutes, they were at the resort and, once again, sorting out accommodations. Alex's crew took over the spaces recently vacated by the active duty SEALs.

Back in the War Room, the hotel had once again provided a buffet. Just as they were finishing brunch, the Department of Homeland Security logo began to spin on the flat screen and conversation ceased.

Silas appeared at the now-familiar desk. "Alex, thanks for picking up the slack. We really don't have much to update. The team here in Washington is working directly with Assistant Police Chief John Winslow. They are checking every house under the guise of warning everyone of the impending hurricane and encouraging them to evacuate. As we identify homes that should be vacant but aren't, he has a second team approaching those homes with the same spiel. If no one answers the door, we are marking it as a possible hideout for Jaja. St. John is a small island, but so is the police force. Alex, if your men are rested, we'd really appreciate it if you would help them."

"We'd be happy to take on that duty, Silas. We all slept last night." The corners of Alex's mouth kicked up. "Why don't you let us check out the homes where the satellites show people who shouldn't be there. We're better-equipped to handle those situations than the local police."

Silas grinned. "Agreed. Dex, I'd like you and your team to grab a few hours of sleep. Be ready to roll in minutes because when we find this fucker, you're going after him."

Dex stifled a yawn. "Thank you, Si. Believe me, sleep would be truly appreciated."

"Gentlemen, you have your assignments. Homeland out." The screen went black just before the homeland security logo reappeared.

"So, Alex, where did you find that old Black Hawk?" Dex asked as he stood.

"We'd hunted down two small sightseeing birds flown by a couple of guys out of St. Croix. They were experienced enough, both with several tours in Afghanistan, but they weren't sure how those light little choppers would do in this kind of wind. They told us about this crazy old guy and his son in Puerto Rico who were rebuilding Black Hawks. We finally found Rodney and Randy Oster." Alex took a sip of his coffee before he continued.

"Rodney flew choppers in Vietnam and some of the first Black Hawks in Grenada, and Randy retired about five years ago from the Army after commanding a Black Hawk squadron." Alex shook his head. "Randy had to practically tie his father down, the old man wanted to come on this mission so bad."

"I'm just glad you found us some transportation off this island," Dex admitted. He looked around the gathering. "I want everybody to move in for introductions."

Each team stood huddled together. Inwardly, Dex smiled. He knew how to make these people talk to each other. "Breaching team, I want you to meet Remi Steel, Flynn O'Rourke, and Gage Ramsey." He looked across the space at Ethan Steadman and Liam Bridger. "They are former SEALs."

Instantly recognizing frog brothers, they genuinely smiled at each other.

Dex moved on. "Jake Jamison and Zeb Fletcher, Special Forces." Immediately the four Army Green Berets from the Department of Justice—William Edge, Stephen Clayborn, Devin Martindale, and Robert Taylor —all grinned.

Moving right along, Dex pointed to the last two men. "This is Nolan Turner, Air Force para-jumper and exceptional medic, and last but not least, Blake Wallace, Marine SpecOps."

"I'd like you to meet my current team." Dex introduced each man, announcing their branch of service. His gaze stopped on Rayne.

A shot of jealousy raced through him. He didn't want her introduced to all these young, virile, available men. It wasn't as though he had any claim on her. Except there was that kiss last night.

He had obviously hesitated too long because when he glanced back at her, she looked furious.

Holding out her hand to the newcomers, she

announced, "I'm Rayne Yoshida, Senior Special Agent with the Secret Service. I'm hoping you've been briefed on the two remaining hostages, Callie and Angelique Sedgwick. They are the daughter and wife of Congressman Robert Sedgwick, the Speaker of the House. I am the agent in charge of his personal protection detail, and I'm here to assist in the rescue of his family. Dex and I worked together over a decade ago in Nigeria capturing several of the highest-ranking members of the Boco Haram." She gave Dex an eat-shit-and-die smile showing two rows of white teeth. "This time, I intend to get that son of a bitch."

All Dex could do was watch as each man on his former team from the Venezuela mission shook her hand. He noticed as several scanned her slight, but powerful, little body. He quelled the need to run over and throw his arms around her, kissing her in front of everyone, declaring she was his.

But she wasn't.

The satellite phone buzzed in his pocket. Checking the caller ID, it was Silas. Before he could get out his name, his boss for this mission started talking. "Don't say a word and don't mention my name. If you're near people, walk far enough away so no one can overhear our conversation."

To anyone who was looking, Dex pointed to the phone, turned his back and walked toward the door. The multiple discussions continued inside the building. Glancing over his shoulder before he stepped outside, he was happy to see that his former team and his new team were bonding. He tried to ignore the fact that several of the men were chatting with Rayne.

"What's up, Si?" Dex asked as soon as he was out of hearing range.

"I want you to have a private discussion with Senior Special Agent Yoshida. See if she has any idea why Jaja would focus on the Sedgwicks, other than the obvious since he is the Speaker of the House. Is there a possibility that they were the target to begin with and everyone else was simply collateral? Jaja was not vacationing on St. John Island and happened to stumble across ten politicians' children. He went there for a purpose. The list of names he gave in the last video seems pretty bullshit to all the analysts here. He also gave up twelve hostages rather easily."

Given the firefight they'd had with the guards, Dex wouldn't exactly consider the rescue easy, but Si was right. It could have been much worse. Jaja could have been killing hostages all along.

"I'll talk to her and get back to you," Dex promised and ended the call. He was looking forward to getting Rayne alone.

CHAPTER TWELVE

Holding out her hand, she said, "It looks like Dex forgot to introduce both you and me. I'm Rayne Yoshida and you are..."

With a gracious smile the handsome Latino held out his hand. "Alex Wolf. I'm the managing partner of Guardian Security." He pointed to the new team. "They all work for me." He glanced toward the now closed door. "Dex does too, on occasion."

"I'm very pleased that you were able to step in and replace the active duty SEALs." She smiled. "Since we are down to two hostages, I understand the Admiral's reasoning for pulling his men. But with the pending storm, it would've been nice to have more search-and-rescue trained men helping us."

"I can assure you, all of my men have the same special operator training as a Navy SEAL, and then some." His grin made her knees weak. Damn, he was good-looking. Far too young for her, but she could still admire an attractive man. "Tell me about Guardian Security."

"We have ten offices across the United States, in most

major cities." He glanced at the chairs. "You've been on your feet all day, let's sit."

Rayne was extremely grateful for the suggestion as she pulled out a chair and sat next to him. Truly wanting to know more about this man, she asked, "what kind of security do you provide?"

"We have several business units including residential, commercial, and personal security. We have active monitoring of homes and businesses and a separate team dedicated to what most consider bodyguards. Our men are available for local as well as international travel."

She didn't miss the word *men*. "You don't have any women in personal protection?"

"We have one. Ryleigh works in our New York City Center." He grinned. "She travels with several regular clients, female corporate officers. Occasionally a client will request someone to accompany his wife, especially in more volatile countries overseas. She and her fiancé, Blake, team up quite often, especially on overseas assignments."

"In ten offices, you only have one woman?" Rayne said accusingly.

Alex looked chastised. "Haven't found the right woman yet."

"I had hoped civilian companies would be more progressive than the federal government." Rayne was disappointed. She had broken a few glass ceilings on the way to becoming a Senior Special Agent with the Secret Service, but she had thought things were different in the civilian world.

Laughter erupted on the other side of the room and she automatically looked in that direction. The teams seemed to have found common ground. She suddenly noticed how young they looked, especially compared to her and Dex. Alex seemed to be older—Rayne had him pegged at around thirty-three—but his mannerisms made him seem a decade older.

Although she was enjoying the conversation, she stifled a yawn. Rayne was dead on her feet.

Alex started to stand. "Rayne, it has been a pleasure talking with you. I apologize, I can tell I'm keeping you from your sleep. I know you were up much of the night."

God bless Alex.

She slowly rose to her feet. "Thank you. And you're right." She glanced over to where the men were clustered. "We all need to get to bed."

She meandered toward the group of men, their broad shoulders filling much of the space. Being small, it wasn't difficult to fit between Devon and Liam.

"Gentlemen, I just wanted to say that I look forward to working with all of you. Hopefully we'll find Callie and Angelique Sedgwick quickly and we can all go home before this hurricane hits." She purposefully looked at the men on the breaching team. "I don't know about you, but I'm going to take Silas Branson's orders seriously and go grab a few hours of sleep."

Stepping outside, she inhaled the damp, salty air that now blew forcefully off the ocean. A gust grabbed the door out of her hand and banged it against the side of the building. Embarrassed, she reached to shut it as the rest of her team exited.

"Rayne, I need to talk to you about the Sedgwicks." Dex seemed to be all business.

"Are you headed to your villa?" She queried.

Dex put his hand on the small of her back. Lightning bolts shot to her nipples and clit. She wondered if Dex would consider having this conversation in her villa. Naked.

Damn. She must be more tired than she thought if her mental and emotional defenses were that far down.

Pulling her aside so Ethan and Liam could get past, he suggested, "Yeah, let's walk and talk."

They gave the two former SEALs space before they headed down the path. Fortunately, they had timed it perfectly between bands of rain. The sun beat down on the storm-soaked sand which almost steamed, thickening the already humid air.

Dex jumped right into the questioning. "Is it possible that Callie and Angelique Sedgwick were Jaja's target from the beginning?"

Rayne shrugged. "Anything is possible, especially since Robert is the Speaker of the House. That's a given."

"The analysts are looking at upcoming legislation that the Congressman may be able to influence, but after that ridiculous list of men Jaja asked to be released, it doesn't seem as though he's interested in something political," Dex noted.

"Jaja had never concerned himself with American politics before," she agreed. "Back when we were first chasing him, he needed money to build his personal army. We damaged his organization for years by capturing his chief financial officer, but he had all those millions he stole through American credit cards. The Secret Service never released the information, but in the end it was calculated to be close to $4.2 million."

"Holy, fuck." Dex seemed to contemplate for a moment before he asked, "Do you think he's after money again?" In the next second, he discarded the idea. "No. If he wanted quick cash, he could've ransomed each one of those hostages for a million dollars apiece. Is Congressman Sedgwick loaded? Wealthier than any of the other politician parents?"

"No. Not at all." Rayne considered all the other children who had been kidnapped. "Violet Russell's mother is a Koch. Her father and uncle are among the top ten richest men in the United States. Sam Russell isn't far behind. He's part of the Mars family, as in the candy fortune. His family is also in the top twenty-five on the Forbes list. Politicians aren't poor, but Robert Sedgwick took a serious hit with his wife's cancer treatment. They tried some experimental and alternative treatments that weren't covered by insurance. He loved Bette and was willing to do anything to save her."

Rayne thought about the deep love between the two that was so evident when she had first started guarding Robert Sedgwick. He had just been elected Speaker of the House when Bette's cancer had returned.

"Are you telling me he doesn't love Angelique and wouldn't do anything to save her?" Dex's question made her think long and hard before she answered.

"I believe he loves her, but I also think Robert's love for Angelique is as different as the women." Rayne glanced up and they were standing in front of the path separating their villas.

"Why don't we finish this inside with a drink?" Given the night they'd just had, she sure as hell could use one. "I hate to call it a nightcap but that's what is going to be for me. I don't care that it's eight-thirty in the morning. I'm sure it will help us both sleep."

"Sure." He gestured for her to lead the way. "Only one. There's no telling how soon they're going to find Jaja and we have to be sharp."

Rayne showed him into the living area and poured them each one finger of scotch from the well-stocked bar. She sat on the couch and he took the chair angled next to it. As she sank into the plush comfort, she let out a long sigh and leaned back. If it weren't for her inquisition, she would have walked into the bedroom and collapsed, clothes and all, onto the bed. She corrected that thought. The boots would come off first. Promising herself that luxury soon, she took a deep breath to chase away the much-wanted sleep.

"Okay, you asked about Robert Sedgwick's wives." She took a sip of the scotch to wet her throat. This could take a while. "Bette and Robert met and fell in love while they were in college. She was working on her master's degree in communications and he was getting his law degree. They were married throughout his entire political career."

Rayne smiled as she thought about the many campaign stories Bette had shared during her convalescence. But Dex only wanted the facts. "During his second campaign for reelection, shortly after Callie was born, Bette was diagnosed with breast cancer. She had a double mastectomy, went through chemo and radiation therapies, and was declared cancer free a few years later. Because congressmen have to be reelected every two years, they were constantly fundraising and campaigning. From what she told me, they were a dynamic team, and I believe it. In the privacy of their home, they were very affectionate, constantly hugging, kissing." Rayne smiled as she confessed, "Even playful ass-grabbing."

She took another sip of her scotch and relished the burn all the way down to her stomach. She had truly liked

Bette Sedgwick and privately mourned her passing. "Shortly after Bette lost another child—she had several miscarriages throughout their marriage, she was diagnosed with stage three ovarian cancer. They got her into some medical trials, but it quickly moved to stage four. Robert asked me once about traveling overseas for nonpolitical purposes, so I know he was looking at alternative treatments in other countries."

A lump formed in Rayne's throat as she thought back to those days. "It was about then, that Bette made the decision she'd had enough. She once told me that God had tried to take her once before, but he knew Callie needed her more, so he gave them those years together."

"So, Callie is their only child," Dex interjected.

"Yeah, but it wasn't for lack of trying. They wanted more children. It just didn't work out for them." Rayne sipped the last of her allotted scotch and got up to rinse out her glass.

As she walked past Dex, he reached out and grabbed her wrist. When she turned to face him, their hands naturally slid together. "Do you want children?"

Laughter burst from somewhere deep inside her. "You don't know much about women do you. That ship has sailed for me." Damn, her defenses were down.

At his look of shock, she decided to educate him. "In case you've forgotten, I'm forty-two years old. Even at age thirty-five, the risk for mother and child are high. For someone my age, there are all kinds of problems. Answering your question, do I want children?" She swallowed hard. "Not anymore."

Dex pulled her into his lap, shocking her speechless. "You know there are other ways to have children. Adop—"

"What adoption agency do you think is going to consider me? I'm a single mother, who works an average of sixty hours a week with no local family support. My job is to be a human shield, prepared to take bullets to protect someone else. Who, in their right mind, would consider me a good candidate to raise a child?" She leaned back to take a good look at him.

He was totally clueless.

She decided to give him a break. "Besides, I've always been career-driven. After growing up in a big family, I wasn't all that interested in having one of my own. Making money that was mine to spend, having a place I didn't have to share with siblings, having peace and quiet was all I wanted when I left home." Tilting her head, she wondered, "How about you? Do you have children? Want them?"

"No kids. Never really wanted them." Dex repositioned her in his lap.

It wasn't until that moment that it dawned on her where she was. Not a place a good team member should ever be, but this was Dex. They were more than team member and team leader.

He continued through clenched teeth. "Kids are nothing but bargaining chips in a divorce, and the divorce rate for SEALs is over ninety percent. I wasn't going to give any woman that kind of control over me."

His declaration threw her for a moment. There were so many things wrong with his statement she didn't know where to begin.

But he just kept talking. "It sounds like the first Mrs. Sedgwick was very supportive of her husband's political life and someone you liked." Dex had totally changed the subject, tossing Rayne out of her train of thought. "You said Angelique is the opposite."

"What I said was that the two women are very different." She took a second to think of examples. "Bette was extremely focused on Callie. Angelique practically ignores the child. Bette knew how to smile and bite her tongue. Angelique just blurts out anything that pops into that tiny brain of hers, then posts it on social media. Robert's office is continually publicly correcting Angelique's statements."

Rayne cringed inwardly. "Here's a perfect example. Shortly after they were married—and remind me to come back to the wedding fiasco—Robert took Angelique on a European junket. The minute she stepped off the plane, she took a selfie and posted on Instagram and Twitter listing every piece of clothing and the designer label. And before you ask, yes. She mentioned which pieces of La Perla lingerie she was wearing. Trust me, his constituents deep in the mountains of Virginia were not pleased with her attempt at southern royalty."

"I take it Bette would never have made such a faux pas." Dex ran his hand up and down her arm, igniting nerve endings that spread prickles of desire through her whole body.

"No. Never. She had class with a real down-to-earth quality about her. Conservative. She knew when to speak and when to keep her mouth closed." Rayne had admired those qualities in Bette.

"I promise we'll come back to the wedding story, but how did Robert end up marrying Angelique? I'm surprised he was attracted to her."

Rayne giggled. "Dex, have you *seen* pictures of this woman? She gives Dolly Parton a run for her money. Big blonde hair, big boobs...No, they're gigantic...and more curves than a Grand Prix racetrack."

"Do I detect a little breast envy?" Dex slipped his hand over her breast, gently massaging, then rubbed his thumb over her nipple.

She gasped in a breath as her nipples instantly hardened and shot a wake-up message to her long-underused clit. No man, since her ex-husband, had touched her so intimately.

Damn. Dex still knew how to play her body.

She should tell him to stop.

Why the hell would she want to do that? He seemed to be enjoying himself and she was certainly appreciating his touch. They were both consenting adults. Very adult. They could have noncommittal sex. Plus, it wouldn't be the first time.

"So, Angelique is a *real looker* as some would say." Dex's voice seemed to come out of nowhere and float through her brain.

Rayne had completely lost her place in the conversation.

"Uhm. Yes. She's quite beautiful. She doesn't have the brains God gave a butterfly, though." *Oops.* Rayne certainly shouldn't be talking this way about the Congressman's wife.

But it was true. And Dex needed to know the truth about Angelique. God only knows what's going to come out of that woman's mouth when she's finally rescued.

Dex nuzzled Rayne's neck. "Damn. You smell good."

She fought the urge to pull away and look at his face, but she really liked what he was doing. "You have to be kidding. I'm still sweaty and I stink."

He licked her neck. "You taste salty." His voice was a low rumble that shook her to her core.

Although she wanted nothing more than to strip him naked and straddled his lap, riding them both to screaming ecstasy, Rayne knew they needed to finish talking about Angelique, then get some rest. "Dex, I need a shower, then we both need some sleep."

He kissed her neck and pulled away. "You're right. Let's finish this talk, then we'll shower and crawl in bed."

She whipped her head to gaze into lust-filled eyes. Certainly he hadn't meant that they were going to shower together then crawl into the same bed, had he? She'd cross that bridge when they came to it.

Needing space, Rayne decided to take the empty scotch glasses to the kitchen. When she went to stand, her hip met his impressive erection. Deep inside she was proud that she was enticing enough to arouse a man like Dex. After the way her ex had blatantly cheated on her, accused her of being emotionless and boring in bed, she had questioned her sex appeal. It was reassuring to know that she still had it.

Grabbing his empty glass off the coffee table, hers was still in her hand, she made her way to the kitchen side of the breakfast bar. She rinsed out the glasses and placed them in the dishwasher. The rote task helped her regain her focus.

Back in control, Rayne was ready to finish answering Dex's questions and then get some much-needed sleep. "You had asked me how Angelique and Robert met."

CHAPTER THIRTEEN

Dex knew he should be concentrating on the possibility that Angelique and Callie Sedgwick were Jaja's primary targets from the beginning, but alone in this private villa with Rayne seemed so intimate, familiar. The two of them, working together, trying to bring down Aahil Mohammed Jaja, it was as though the past twelve years hadn't happened.

Hoping they could finish this interview soon, Dex was ready to move on to the shower, then the bed. The idea of running soapy hands over Rayne's entire body, paying special attention to each breast, then thoroughly cleaning the nest of jet-black hair at the apex of her thighs, was making his erection throb with every heartbeat.

It was a damn good thing she got up from his lap to deal with the dishes while he dealt with his unruly dick. He hadn't been this turned on in years.

Rayne grabbed two bottles of water from the fridge and headed back. He was a little peeved when she skirted around the coffee table, out of his reach, but Dex figured she may need a little space as well. Two minutes ago, while he fondled her breast, her breathing had become erratic. He'd bet his next paycheck that if he had slipped a finger between her wet folds, her clit would be hard and begging.

She dropped onto the sofa, once again, before handing him a bottle of chilled water. After a long drink, she glanced his way. He simply watched her, waiting for the rest of the story, or an invitation to continue this later as they headed straight to the shower.

But he needed this information first. Maybe he'd pick up something that she and her team missed while vetting Angelique Johnson Sedgwick.

Finally, she spoke. "You had asked me how Angelique and Robert met. During Robert's most recent run for Congress, Angelique showed up as a volunteer in the Roanoke office. All she was truly qualified to do was stuff envelopes and make voter encouragement phone calls."

Rayne sipped her water. "When we vetted her, the campaign coordinator at that office told us that Angelique only came to work when Robert was scheduled to be there. She fawned all over the man, sticking her boobs out toward him every chance she got, pawing his arm as she told him how much she enjoyed working for his campaign. I was close to the point where I usually pulled Congressman Sedgwick away and someone on my team moved in to block her."

She paused for a long moment. "Looking back, I pegged her that day as a potential troublemaker. Brian, my second-in-command, mentioned that Angelique's accent was fake. He'd know, because he was born and raised in Western Virginia."

Taking another sip, Rayne continued, "That night, at

a fund-raising dinner, somehow Angelique ended up in the seat right next to the congressman—wearing a dress so low-cut that my team was taking bets if, and when, her nipples were going to pop out."

Dex loved how straightforward Rayne could be. Sometimes, he would forget that she was a woman because she acted so much like the men around him, and the next moment she could be soft and supple, very feminine. Like a rogue wave hitting him while swimming in the middle of the ocean, he realized he preferred women with strong personalities.

That's why he and his first wife, Jan, didn't make it. Rayne wouldn't have any problem with him being gone for long periods of time, and she could handle the problem, without four phone calls, when the washing machine broke down. She would also be loyal, unlike Genevieve, his second wife. He hadn't been gone ten days when one of his buddies back in Virginia Beach had called him after seeing her leave a local club in the arms of another man.

No. Rayne would take care of her own needs. He wondered how many vibrators she owned. He glanced toward the bedroom. Had she brought one with her? Playing with toys could be fun for them both. Her voice brought his gaze, and attention, back to the woman who continued to fascinate him.

"Angelique dragged Robert onto the dance floor several times, positioning herself next to him as he made the grin-and-grip rounds. Until we started the vetting process, we had no idea that the Roanoke coordinator hadn't set that up. Our job is purely security and has nothing to do with his campaign except to ensure the venues are secure," she explained.

Rayne sipped more water and looked as though she just wanted to close her eyes and fall asleep. He'd get her to bed soon enough. He, too, was fighting sleep.

Taking a deep breath, she leaned forward, placing her elbows on her knees. "The next night, she showed up in Lexington. She couldn't worm her way onto the stage that night, but she did manage to dance with him several times. Once again, she was hanging on his elbow as he greeted local dignitaries. I was able to ask him if he wanted us to remove her, and he claimed she was harmless, so we backed off."

"Let me guess, she showed up in his hotel room one night?" Dex offered. He had that happen to him in Dubai. He'd been flirting with the female Navy pilot who had flown them from the ship for a few days of R and R. When he'd returned to his room after 4x4 dune bashing and sand boarding, he'd found her naked in his bed. They enjoyed three days, and three fuck-fabulous nights together, before parting ways.

"Close, but not quite." Rayne's lips pulled into a straight line. "She tried, though. Our protocol always includes an agent in the congressman's room after it's been cleared of bugs, even when it's empty. You would be amazed at how many people walk into unoccupied but rented hotel rooms."

"So, how did she weasel her way into his bedroom?" Dex held her gaze. He was getting a bad feeling about Angelique. He knew her type.

"She kept showing up at his campaign stops, especially in the western side of the state. One night, just as the congressman was about to go upstairs to his hotel room, she asked to speak with him privately. We knew he was in a hurry because when he was on the road without

Callie, he would call her every single night before she went to bed. It also made a great excuse for him to leave a party."

Rayne chugged the last of her water. "So, Angelique walked with him to the elevator. We were all about to step in and separate them, but Robert waved us off. When we made it to his room and the agent inside opened the door for him, Angelique started crying, insisting she speak with him alone about a very personal matter. He invited her in. She didn't leave until the morning. I can assure you, her walk of shame was one of pride." Rayne grimaced. "The agent outside the door said she was a screamer."

Rayne looked at the empty bottle as though she wanted another. "It didn't take long before Angelique tried ordering his security detail around, claiming that she and Robert needed privacy. Within three months, shortly after he was elected, they were married in one of the biggest weddings I've ever seen. Security was a fucking nightmare. Angelique had everyone invited from the Queen of England to the President. Thankfully, most of the International delegates declined."

Scowling, she continued. "The bad news was that over a hundred from his side of the House, dozens of senators, the President, and several international diplomats, showed up. And talk about bridezilla. Angelique was a fucking nightmare to deal with. She kept firing the wedding planners, and each new one wanted to make major changes, all affecting security. I finally had a conversation with Robert, who seemed to be more in lust than in love, but at least he had some control over her."

Rayne let out a heavy sigh and slowly shook her head side to side. "That bitch didn't want Callie in the wedding. Robert insisted, though."

152 | KALYN COOPER

Dex's eyebrows knitted together. "You've indicated before that Angelique and Callie don't get along. Why the hell did the woman come on this trip with Callie?"

Rayne shrugged. "I have no idea. She decided at the very last minute she was going to go, and no one could talk her out of it. Robert thought it might be a bonding experience for them, so he didn't discourage her."

A niggling started in the recesses of Dex's mind. It could be something. Or not. "How did Robert integrate Angelique into his home and Callie's life?"

Rayne huffed. "He didn't. The only time he ever brought Angelique into his home was when Callie was spending the night with a friend." Once again, she shook her head. "The first couple times she was there, if Robert was on the phone in his study, my team found her wandering around the house opening drawers, looking in cabinets, snooping. I'm not talking about the kitchen where she might be preparing a meal, or even a snack. I'm being honest here when I tell you, I'm not sure the woman knows how to serve cheese and crackers."

Dex grinned. As he and Rayne had worked many long nights together in Nigeria, often in his room or hers, she would get up in the middle of a conversation and throw together an elaborate plate that included several types of cheese, four or five different kinds of crackers, and any colorful fruit available in the refrigerator. Sometimes it was a meal. Sometimes it was a snack. To this day, his refrigerator contained at least ten different kinds of cheeses and a drawer filled with fresh fruit. Since their time together, he had discovered several new kinds of crackers. He'd also learned to *man cook*.

"I take it you don't approve of Angelique," he stated.

"No." She said emphatically. "My whole team

agreed that she was nothing but a gold-digging social climber. A stupid one at that, proven when we vetted her. She barely made it through high school, although she was very popular with the boys. Not a single member of my team felt good about her, but it's not our place to tell the Speaker of the House who he can date."

The edges of Rayne's pretty mouth turned down. "My second-in-command, Brian, tried though. He'd overseen the vetting process, but Robert didn't seem to care about her many lies. Did I tell you that she didn't even invite her own parents to her wedding? I was in the meeting with the wedding planner when she claimed her parents were dead. They're very much alive and living in West Virginia."

Narrowing his eyes, Dex clarified, "So she's an adept liar. And Congressman Sedgwick was willing to overlook this?" At that moment, he wasn't sure who was dumber, the congressman or his trophy wife. Or if Angelique was sly as a fox and an Oscar-worthy actress?

Rayne yawned as she nodded in agreement. "Unfortunately, yes."

Not trusting Angelique Sedgwick at that point, he wondered if she had any connection to Jaja. "I'm going to run next door and grab my tablet. I want you to look at a few pictures and tell me if you've ever seen Angelique with any of these people." As he stood, he scanned her sexy but dirty body. "It may take a few minutes to download the pictures, so why don't you shower while I'm gone?"

Deep appreciation crossed her pretty face. "Take your time. I intend to enjoy every minute of the hot pounding spray."

Hot. Pounding. The words bounced around in his brain as he thought of Rayne naked in the shower.

No. He chastised his body as he stood. Finish this. Then we'll play.

Before he could reach out and grab Rayne, pulling her to him and kissing her mindless, he spun on his booted heel and headed to the door.

"If you take too long, I'll come get you from the shower." He glanced back over his shoulder before he stepped outside. He gave her his panty-dropping grin. "Or I'll join you."

Dex didn't miss the lust that flashed in her deep brown eyes just before he closed the door.

Although he was right next door, the dense vegetation forced him to go down her path then up to his villa. It gave him just enough time to place a call to Silas and share this new information. They'd talked previously about possible DC connections to Jaja and by the time Dex had his tablet turned on, the analysts were already filling a file on the secure server.

"Silas, is it possible to find out if the Sedgwicks and anyone on this list ever attended the same party?" Dex thought it was a long shot, but he couldn't ignore the possibility.

"Let me see what we can find." Silas then switched subjects. "We've already checked out about a third of the island. This is important, but both you and Rayne need sleep. Make that happen. Homeland out."

As soon as the mission coordinator hung up, Dex's tablet started to flash with downloads.

When he arrived back at Rayne's villa, she didn't answer his initial knock. Twisting the doorknob, he was pleased to discover it was unlocked. "Rayne, sweetheart,

I'm back," he called loud enough so she could hear him in the bedroom.

"I'll be right out." A few seconds later, she strode through the door, cinching the belt on the complimentary resort hotel robe. It was large on her petite frame and opened slightly as she sat down on the couch and crossed her legs at the knee, exposing several inches of toned thigh.

Fuck. How was he ever going to make it through the next few minutes as they perused the pictures, knowing that she was completely naked underneath the white fluffy robe?

He tried looking down. When did her little feet and red painted toenails become so fucking sexy?

Forcing his gaze to her face, he noticed a few fan lines near the outer edges of her eyes. She still looked delicate, like a china doll, or in her case, a Japanese doll. Free of all makeup, she was gorgeous. Large, almond shaped eyes, perfectly arched black eyebrows still wet from the shower, light smooth skin unmarred by the sun, yet tinged pink over her cheeks from the heat of her shower. He had no words to describe her beauty.

His. That's what he wanted. The awareness of just how much he desired this woman filled him, and his cock.

"Okay, what do you have?" Rayne looked up at him expectantly.

A dick as hard as a rock that I'd love for you to take in that pretty little mouth of yours, he thought as he stood in front of her, his erection practically staring her in the face.

He quickly sat down next to her and pulled up the first picture. "These are all known contacts of Jaja, currently in the USA. Let me know if you recognize anyone, even if you think you may have seen them at a party or event."

Taking the tablet, she began flipping through pictures. "I've seen this man several times," she declared. He was an aide to the ambassador from Chad.

"Do you remember ever seeing Angelique talking with him?" Dex pressed.

Rayne shrugged. "At these events, we're concentrating on anyone who could be a potential threat to the life of Congressman Sedgwick. I tend to ignore Angelique as much as possible. But I do remember this man talking to Robert recently, within the last month to six weeks."

Dex clicked on the information icon. "Well, isn't that a coincidence. It seems he is a distant relative of the prisoner in Chad that Jaja wants released." Dex didn't believe in coincidences. He marked that one as a possibility and clicked on the icon to send it directly to the analysts.

She scanned through several more pictures until she stopped and stared once again. "He looks familiar, but I'm not sure why. There's something not quite right about the picture."

Once again expanding the information, they had an aha moment at the same time.

"Damn. He certainly does look like his father," Rayne noted.

Dex and Rayne had chased Usman, Aahil Mohammed Jaja's older brother, for nearly a month. He was credited masterminding the $4.2 million credit card heist. His master's degree from Stanford in computer science, and a blatant despise for Americans, made him the primary suspect.

The man in the picture could have been a younger version of Usman. Faruq was about to finish his undergraduate degree—surprise, surprise—in computer science, at Massachusetts Institute of Technology, and had already been accepted into the school's master's degree program. His picture got flagged and with the click of a button, it was sitting in a hot box at Homeland Security.

There were a few more pictures that Rayne took an extra few minutes to examine.

She yawned as she came to the end of the photographs.

They still had nothing definite, but plenty of leads.

Dex placed his palm on Rayne's cheek. Leaning in slowly, he brushed his lips across hers. "Thank you, sweetheart, you did well."

She slid his tablet onto the coffee table and grabbed his head with both her small hands. Pulling him back to her, she kissed him hard and long. Their tongues dueled as he traced his fingertips down the pounding pulse line in her neck. He slid his hand under the soft robe and caressed each bare breast, tracing the underside with a finger.

Just like she'd done twelve years ago, she gasped in a breath and squeezed her knees together. *Oh, yes.* She was as turned on as him. His heart was racing, and he was panting as though he had just completed the annual physical fitness test.

He needed to make sure she understood that this was a onetime event. He couldn't offer her any more than an immediate release. That's all he expected of her as well. She had betrayed him once. He would never give her the chance to do that again.

Pulling back, he gave himself a few seconds to catch his breath. "You know I want you, but I need you to understand this is just sex. A stress reliever. We're not picking up where we left off in Nigeria."

"Nigeria had been great, until you—"

"No. We're not going to go there." He didn't want to hear more of her lies. All he wanted, no, needed, was her gorgeous body. And she needed his. "Promise me. Just sex."

"I promise." Then the glint returned to her eyes. "Now kiss me and touch me until I fall apart in your arms."

Thank Christ that she was on board with this plan. He leaned down and kissed her, never releasing her mouth, he untied the belt. Gently kneading her breasts, he rolled her nipples in unison between his thumbs and forefingers. He was positive she didn't realize that she was arching into him offering him more. When he pinched her hardened nipples, she bit his lower lip and rocked her hips toward him.

Breaking the kiss, he gently laid her back on the couch as he kissed his way down. He concentrated for a few moments on each breast before continuing his path over her flat stomach, to the black curls he'd dreamed of last night.

His shoulders were a tight fit on the couch, so he picked up her legs, licking the inside of her thighs as he spread them wide, making his way to her glistening folds. He ran the tip of his tongue the length of her slit, not wanting to miss a drop of her feminine essence, before he used his thumbs to open her to him.

When he kissed her clit, her hips shot off the couch.

Oh, yes. He remembered how much she loved it when

he licked and sucked her to orgasm. Lapping up her juices, he then concentrated on the hard bundle of nerves that had swollen under his ministrations. He slid two fingers into her and curled them, finding the G spot, rubbing it as he sucked her clitoris.

Her walls contracted and spasmed around his fingers, assuring him she was close. Her legs tightened, threatening to crush his head, but he persisted.

"Dex." She sucked in a ragged breath. "I want you..." Gasp. "Inside me. Now."

He slowly traveled his gaze up her gorgeous body until their eyes met. He wiggled his fingers, stroking that special spot. "I am inside you."

"You fucking know what I mean," she said through a clenched jaw.

"Not this time, sweetheart. This is all about you." Dex knew she was close and took her clit into his mouth and sucked hard, rubbing his tongue over the bottom as he increased the pressure on the rough spot inside her channel.

Rayne's whole body shook as she came. He loved the uncontrolled noises that she made. He stayed with her, pumping his fingers until she lay unmoving.

He pulled his fingers out and stuffed them in his mouth, wanting to taste every bit of her.

Gently sliding from between her limp legs, he stood, drinking in every inch of her bare body splayed before him. He promised himself in that moment that they would do this again, and again. He would slide into her from this very position, take her on her knees from behind, let her ride him as he fondled her breasts, and any other position they could figure out.

Then they would eat cheese and crackers between bites of fruit.

She purred as she rolled on her side. She was sound asleep.

He couldn't leave her there, so he gently gathered her in his arms and put her to bed, pulling the light comforter over her.

Kissing her sweetly, he stepped away, turned out the light and trotted to his villa.

His cock pulsing and threatening to give him one of the worst case of blue balls he'd ever had, he stepped into the shower. With a hand filled with soapsuds, he closed his eyes and leaned against the marble, picturing her bobbing head sucking him off as he squeezed his fist and rubbed up and down his straining cock. A couple swipes of his thumb over the sensitive tip and he shook with relief.

Finishing his shower quickly, he crawled naked into bed, wishing that he was curled up with the woman next door.

The alarm went off.

Damn. He had a wake-up.

The alarm went off again.

No. That's not an alarm. That's an old-fashioned phone. He would never have such an obnoxious ring tone on his cell.

He cracked his eyes enough to find the hotel phone on the nightstand. "Yeah."

"It's Alex. I think we found them."

Dex bolted up in bed, wide awake.

CHAPTER FOURTEEN

Callie sat on the opposite end of the ugly red couch from the Step-Monster, curling up into a ball and trying to be as small as possible. She was so glad her wrists and ankles were no longer tied together.

Looking around their new location, Callie wondered if the owners of this house were from the Middle East. She'd seen the deep red rugs, burgundy and gold pillows, and the unique design on the curtains when they had traveled in Turkey. She and her mom would travel quite often with her father. Her dad would meet with politicians, and she and her mother got to play tourist. But that was before her mother got sick.

Tears threatened to burst as more memories of her mom played through her mind. Callie glared toward the other end of the couch where the SHREW sat. That was the new name that she, Charlotte, and Brynn came up with. It stood for Stupid Hateful Rotten Evil Woman. They all agreed it fit Angelique perfectly.

Callie wondered when they were going to bring the

other girls and chaperones over to this new house. So far, it was just her and the *B* with an *itch*.

She'd been so scared when they took her away.

Tucked up next to Charlotte, sound asleep, someone had yanked her out of the makeshift bed. Her feet weren't even touching the floor as Grunt dragged her to one of the back bedrooms and threw her on the box springs. It was hard and she banged her elbow.

He was going to rape her; she just knew it. Why else would they bring her, alone, back here? She tried to scream but the only thing that came out were whimpers.

A second man walked into the room carrying plastic strings.

It didn't take a genius to realize they were going to tie her to that bed, then they were both going to rape her. She was a good girl. Still a virgin. But maybe that's why they wanted her.

The two men started talking to each other in that language she didn't understand.

Maybe while they are distracted, I could sneak away.

She tried to quietly scramble off the other side of the bed and stay low, but the second man caught her and yanked her elbows behind her back. Grunt grabbed her legs.

Kicking as hard as she could, Callie couldn't seem to connect with anything but air. He was too strong. Moving faster than she'd seen the guard move before, he had her ankles bound together with the plastic zip ties. The other man started to tie her hands behind her back when Mr. Jaja walked into the room. He yelled a few orders then stood in front of her.

"If you promise to be cooperative, they can tie your hands in front. Tied behind your back can be very uncomfortable and we have quite a drive to make." He grabbed her chin and made her look at him. "Are you going to do as we ask or fight every inch of the way like your mother? That bitch."

"She's not my mother. She's just some stupid idiot who tricked my father into getting married." Callie knew the minute she said the words that it was a bad move on her part.

Ms. Rogers had reviewed what to do when kidnapped. *Be cooperative.*

As contrite as possible, she looked into the black eyes of her kidnapper. "I'm sorry I said those things, Mr. Jaja. I promise to do whatever you tell me to. Just, please don't hurt me." She glanced over at Grunt and the other man. "Don't let them hurt me."

He wiped a tear away from her cheek with his coal-black finger. "No. You are too valuable to me to let them stain you."

He barked at them in that other language before he bound her wrists together in the front using zip ties once again. "Remember your promise. Liars get punished."

Grunt picked her up with one arm under her knees and the other around her back, then carried her to the repair man's van. He laid her gently on the hard metal floor in the back. Even in the darkness, she recognized Angelique trussed up and gagged on the floor next to her. Grunt climbed in and shut the doors behind him. This time, he sat on the floor, his rifle on his lap.

Mr. Jaja jumped into the passenger side as Dreds slid behind the wheel. It seemed like hours that they bumped along the curvy road before stopping in front of another large house. There were no exterior security lights, so Callie could see very little as Grunt carried her inside. This time, she was placed on a soft comfortable bed.

Mr. Jaja took only one step inside the door. "You will sleep. You will not try to escape. My men have surrounded this house. Yelling for help is useless. There is no one around for miles. If you keep your promise to me, then I will keep my promise to you. My men will not touch you or hurt you. Do I have your word?"

She nodded then squeaked out, "Yes."

"Excellent."

As he turned to leave, she called out, "Mr. Jaja, may I...I need to use the ladies' room."

Walking toward her, he reached in his pocket and flipped out a six-inch blade.

She tried to inchworm her way up the bed.

"Stop," he ordered.

She froze.

"Hold still, child, as I cut your bonds." With a flick of his wrist, she was free once again. He pointed to one of the doors on the far wall. "Bathroom is in there." His hand whipped out and grabbed her chin. "Do I need to remind you of your promise?"

"Na...no, sir, Mr. Jaja." She glanced toward the bathroom door and wondered if he was going to stand there and watch her pee like he had made Ms. Rogers do back at the other houses.

"You are free to move about this bedroom and bathroom. I won't tie you up again unless it's necessary." As he reached the door, he spoke with someone in the hall before turning back toward her. "There are guards everywhere. You cannot escape. If you wish to enjoy the freedom of movement, don't even try." Without warning he disappeared.

Callie had never appreciated the solitude of the bathroom before, but she certainly did then. She was so exhausted that she stumbled back into the bedroom. Pulling the comforter back, she was disappointed to discover the bed had no sheets. Not caring in that moment, she made a sleeping bag out of the comforter. With the soft bed, quiet house, and Mr. Jaja's promise of safety, Callie fell asleep.

The smell of coffee and cooking food awakened her. Although not rested, she was certainly hungry. A glance through the window showed gray, rainy, early-morning light. After using the restroom and washing her face, she sneaked to the door. When she peeked into the hall, Grunt bellowed in that other language.

Mr. Jaja appeared at the far end of the hall. "You may come Ms. Sedgwick. We have food for you." He quickly spoke to Grunt, who didn't move when she walked toward Mr. Jaja.

Callie dared a quick glance over her shoulder into the other bedroom where Angelique lay without a blanket, her hands and ankles still cuffed. The woman often slept till nearly noon, so she doubted she would have to endure the presence of Non-Mom for several hours.

Partway through her surprisingly good breakfast of scrambled eggs mixed with some kind of mystery meat and fresh fruit, Grunt strong-armed Angelique into the room.

"Eat." Mr. Jaja commanded.

Angelique sneered at the dishes on the table and wrinkled her nose. "I don't eat that kind of food."

Callie simply rolled her eyes and forked another piece of mango. Out of the corner of her eye, she saw Mr. Jaja flick his fingers. Grunt yanked Angelique and she stumbled.

"Maybe I'll have a piece of fruit," the Step-Witch blurted as Grunt tried to pull her into the living room.

When Angelique sat down, Callie couldn't remember them ever eating breakfast together. As she thought about it, there was only the tense supper when her dad first introduced her to Angelique, and maybe one other time the three of them had all sat at the same table—but never had the two of them eaten at the same time.

Neither said a word, least of all to each other.

When Callie finished, she stood and glanced at the dirty plates on the table. "Mr. Jaja, may I put these plates in the dishwasher?"

He stared at her for a long moment. Callie wondered if she'd spilled food on her disheveled pajamas. She was working on day two in the same clothes, which felt grungy. She was used to coming home from school and immediately changing out of her uniform. Sometimes she'd go for a swim in their pool, or just throw on a clean pair of jeans and a shirt. Then she changed again for bed. She had never worn the same clothes this long in her life and hoped she would never be in the situation to do it again.

"Good girl," Mr. Jaja praised before sliding a glance toward Angelique, who sat back in her kitchen chair glaring at Callie as the girl collected the dirty plates and silverware from the table.

As soon as the dishes were rinsed and placed in the dishwasher, Mr. Jaja announced, "We are going to the living room and make the video."

Once again, Grunt took Angelique by the arm and

pulled her into the next room, shoving her down on the ugly red couch.

Pacing in front of them, Mr. Jaja asked, "Who does Congressman Sedgwick love more?" His gaze moved from Callie to Angelique. "His new wife? Or his daughter?"

Callie wasn't going to answer that question, because she couldn't. Before Angelique had come along, she had always been sure of her father's love. Even after her mother's death, when her father threw himself into his work and reelection, she never questioned his love for her. But after he married the Barbie Wannabe, he hadn't spent near as much time with her. She wasn't sure Mr. Jaja really wanted the answer to his question, so she sat there and said nothing.

The terrorist leader stepped close to Angelique and leaned down so their faces were on the same level. "You are young and of childbearing age." He glanced toward Callie, then returned his attention to the woman who was only twelve years older. "He can have more worthless daughters. Perhaps you can even give him a son who would be worthy of such a powerful man. Maybe several sons."

"I'm not going to have any children." Angelique sneered at Callie. "She's more than enough for Robert and me. You can take her and let me go free. You don't want me. You want the little virgin."

Callie's jaw dropped. All she could do was stare at the Step-Monster who just tried to give her away to save her own sorry ass.

Mr. Jaja sneered at Angelique. "No, I don't want you, but I'm stuck with you. You were supposed to meet my son at the party two nights ago and tell him when the IRS was converting to the new computer system."

Angelique looked stricken, and scared. "He's your son?"

Callie couldn't believe her step-mother was working with these men. And Angelique was supposed to give them information about the IRS computer system? Was she that big of an idiot? Or was she a spy?

Mr. Jaja's smile was pure evil. "Now, you can tell *me*, wife of the Speaker of the House, when is the IRS converting to the new computer system? Tomorrow? The day after? We know that it's sometime within the next four days. They need to run the third quarter reports on the new system, and they have less than a week to do that."

"I don't know when that's going to happen," she confessed.

"Then you lied to my son, you fucking bitch."

Jaja backhanded Angelique. Her head bounced off the back of the couch. "You thought you could get away by running here?" His mouth twisted in an ugly way. "You're more stupid than we thought. You were so easy to find."

Angelique looked away.

"Do you think your husband knows?"

She looked hopeful as she answered, "I'm sure he does."

"Let's ask him." Jaja whipped out his phone and looked back and forth between Angelique and Callie. "I'm sure you know how to record a video. I've seen plenty of yours online." He handed his phone to Angelique, then grabbed Callie off the couch.

He wrapped his muscular arm around her neck and held her tightly. "Let me know when you're ready to record."

Mr. Jaja held a gun to her head.

Callie's whole body began to shake. She couldn't control it. Jaja was going to kill her and send the video to her dad. Her poor father. He had been through so much. First losing Mom, and now she was going to be dead, too. She was going to miss her dad.

The Witch with a B had a huge smile on her face as she announced, "Go ahead."

"Good morning Congressman Sedgwick. As you can see, I have your daughter. I'm sure you won't miss her because she's just a female. Perhaps your new wife can give you a boy, or two or three."

Angelique screamed from behind the phone, "I told you, we're not having children. I don't want any kids."

No. Angelique didn't even want the child that came with her marriage. Well, if this was the last thing her father was going to see, at least Callie was going to tell him the truth.

"Your wife is a fool and so are you if you listen to her." Jaja was practically screaming in Callie's ear. "You need to fuck her until she's pregnant or find a woman who can give you boys."

"Daddy, you heard her, she doesn't want children. She got rid of my little brother or sister while you were gone. I know you married her because she was pregnant, but she had an abortion while you were traveling. She lied to you about having a miscarriage."

"You fucking little *bitch*," Angelique screamed as she held the cell phone camera pointed toward Callie and Mr. Jaja. "Did you steal my cell phone and listen to my messages?"

"Yes. Just like you listen in on conversations Daddy has on the house phone. And just like you check his voicemail while he's in the shower." Callie only hoped that Mr. Jaja actually sent this video to her father. Maybe then he would realize what a terrible woman he had married.

"Go ahead and shoot her," Angelique encouraged.

Mr. Jaja shook his head and ran the barrel of the gun down Callie's cheek. "She's far too valuable to me. How valuable is she to you, Congressman Sedgwick? All I need from you is a date and a time. Five minutes after you receive this video, I'm going to call you. You're going to tell me exactly what I want to know about the IRS computer conversion, or I'm going to kill one of the two females in your life. Who do you love more? That pretty new wife of yours? Or this?"

He jerked Callie up and ground the muzzle of the gun to her head. It really hurt, but she was madder at Angelique than Jaja.

"Daddy, please, don't do it." Callie understood that if her father gave that information to Jaja, he would be committing treason and he'd go to jail. She wasn't sure which was worse, for her to be dead or all alone in the world.

She looked at her stepmother and suddenly realized that if her father were dead or in prison, Step-Monster would be her only guardian.

Callie would rather be dead than stuck with that woman the rest of her life. "Please, Daddy, you can't commit treason for me. You'll go to jail for the rest of your life because Angelique told Mr. Jaja's son about the computers."

Tears streamed down her face. It felt like she could hardly get the words out. She didn't know if it was how tight Mr. Jaja was holding her or if something in her throat had swollen, shutting off her air.

But she had to let her dad know. "He's going to kill me anyway, Daddy, so please, don't tell him anything...I'm not worth it." Barely above a whisper, she croaked out, "I love you, Daddy. I'll be okay. I'll be with Mom in heaven."

"You have exactly five minutes to think about it, Congressman Sedgwick."

CHAPTER FIFTEEN

Rayne stared at the screen, her fists tightly balled, wanting to punch someone or reach out to the brave young lady she'd grown to love.

"He's going to kill me anyway, Daddy." Callie's words, and her innocent realization evident in those pretty blue eyes, shot daggers into Rayne's heart.

"I'm not worth it." With every crack in her small voice, another fissure split Rayne's heart. She didn't bother to wipe away the tears that rivered down her face and dripped off her jaw. She wanted to take Callie into her arms and do everything within her power to show that child how wonderful a person she was to the depths of her soul.

"I'll be with Mom in heaven."

Yes. Callie's soul would certainly go to heaven, but Rayne wasn't going to let that happen. Not now. That little girl had an entire lifetime ahead of her.

Bette's funeral, and the first time Rayne ever held and comforted Callie, flashed through her mind. There had been legitimate death threats against the Speaker of the

House. It was going to be a very big, public funeral. As a representative from Virginia, thousands of constituents were close enough to drive to their hometown of Lynchburg.

During the final viewing, which was the hour before the funeral, Callie had disappeared. Fearing someone had kidnapped her, Rayne had dispersed her team. She was the one to find the ten-year-old leaning on the backside of a huge old oak tree. After notifying the rest of her team and ordering them back to primary security, Rayne had simply sat on the ground beside the girl.

"Too much for you?" Rayne asked.

Without looking at her, Callie said, "The flowers stink."

Rayne had to admit, "They are overpowering, aren't they?"

"Those people didn't know my mom." Callie sniffed back a tear. "They just say nice things to my dad, so he'll vote the way they want him to."

Jaded and barely a decade old. Already despising lobbyists.

"That's true of many, but there are several people here who knew and loved your mom. Congressman and Mrs. Thompson just went through the line. They asked about you." That was the moment of panic when the Secret Service realized Callie was gone.

"There was a woman who was your mom's roommate in college. By hiding out here you missed those stories. Another lady lived next door to your mom when she was your age. Several men and women who knew your mother told about the wonderful things your Mom did for them. By sitting out here, you're missing all of that." Rayne hoped she was getting through to the little girl.

"But I miss my mom." Callie broke into tears.

Rayne pulled the small-framed child into her lap and held her as she cried, reassuring as much as she could. About fifteen minutes later, Brian's voice came through her earpiece—Congressman Sedgwick was concerned and wanted Callie with him.

The young girl had made it through the day. But that night, she cried in Rayne's arms once again. Several times over the next few months, she and Callie would spend quiet, private time together. She had become somewhere between a mother figure, older sister, and adult friend—a place Rayne had never been before.

Jaja's final words on the video brought her back to the present.

With tears still running down her cheeks, Rayne vowed, "I'm going to kill the fucker."

"You'll have to stand in line," Dex stated through clenched teeth.

Mart sobbed uncontrollably in her husband's arms. "That's the Gunderson's home." She sniffed and wiped away tears. Stomping to the map laid out on the table, she jabbed a perfectly manicured fingernail toward a house.

"I have to make sure you're absolutely positive, Mart," Dex pressed

"I'd recognize that disgusting red and gold brocade couch anywhere." The real estate agent cringed, then pulled her tablet out of her beach bag-sized purse. She had the interior shots of the home pulled up within seconds. Mart took over the controls on Dex's laptop, rewinding to the opening shot of Jaja holding Callie at gunpoint in the middle of the living room.

Laying the two devices side-by-side, everyone gathered around to compare. It was a match.

"I didn't even see the couch," Dex confessed. "And this place was already on our list."

"I'm sorry, we hadn't gotten to that one yet," Alex apologized.

"No problem," Dex reassured. "I called you back here for a reason."

"Do you want my team to go there first?" Alex offered.

"No. This was sent to Congressman Sedgwick less than ten minutes ago so it's highly likely they're still there." His gaze swept the room. "I'd appreciate your backup, though."

"You've got it." Alex nodded.

"Breaching gear. Meet at the SUVs in five minutes," Dex ordered.

Rayne was one of the first through the door, headed toward her villa. A warm hand touched her back and sent awareness through her body.

Dex.

"You don't have to do this. You can stay in the war room and coordinate," Dex offered in a warm and concerned voice.

Still striding toward her room, she glared at him over her shoulder. "Like fuck I'll stay here. And I swear to God, if I get the chance, he's dead. He's got Callie."

"He also has Angelique," Dex reminded her.

"That traitorous fucking bitch can die as far as I'm concerned. I will personally see to it that she is tried for treason when we get back to Virginia." Rayne was a tank on the roll. She intended to crush anything, and everyone, who got in her way.

"You. Are. Mad," Dex noted. "I haven't heard you

swear this much since we left the office in Nigeria that night we took down Jaja's upper echelon."

"I wasn't anywhere near this angry back then. This time, that fucker is going down." That was a promise as far as Rayne was concerned.

Her phone rang. Checking the ID, she saw it was Brian. "Talk to me," she ordered her second-in-command. "I just saw the video. How is Robert taking it?"

"Congressman Sedgwick was devastated. For a moment there, we thought he was having a heart attack. Thankfully, some of the senior members of the FBI kidnap team were at the house. One of those guys was a paramedic. It took us three full minutes to get the congressman calmed down so we could prepare strategy for Jaja's call."

"What did he tell Jaja?" Rayne turned left as the path split but Dex followed her.

"Once we get inside, put it on speaker," Dex demanded.

Throwing open the door, Rayne strode straight to her bedroom. She clicked on the speaker and laid her phone on the nightstand. "Brian, I have you on speaker and mission commander Dex Carson is with me. Thanks to the video, we believe we know their location."

"Excellent." Brian acknowledged. "We had Silas Branson on the line advising us before Jaja called. On his advice, the congressman gave Jaja the wrong date. He obviously has a second source. He indicated that if Congressman Sedgwick had lied to him, he was going to kill one of the hostages in six hours."

Six hours? Rayne whipped her gaze to Dex. He hadn't said anything in the briefing about a time limit. Her glare was answered by a single nod.

"We'll get him before then," Dex reassured. "Homeland has identified his son, who was working under a different name at the Chad Embassy. They've agreed to turn him over to our custody. They should be picking him up any minute. The noose is tightening on Jaja. We're going to get him this time."

"Rayne," Brian sounded hesitant. "We're heading your way."

Rayne picked up her bulletproof vest and paused. "Exactly what do you mean, you're heading my way?"

"Congressman Sedgwick has insisted on coming down there. Nothing is going to keep him from his daughter." Brian huffed. "At this moment, he wants to personally kill his wife. He's already called his attorney to start divorce proceedings and the Attorney General to draw up treason charges. I have never seen the man this angry or determined. He's charted a private jet to take us to St. Thomas."

"Don't you *dare* let him come to St. John," Rayne threatened. "I don't want him anywhere near Jaja or his followers. Does Robert understand that we're facing a hurricane?"

"Yes, ma'am." Brian sounded like he was walking outdoors. "He doesn't care. He wants to be there when *you* hand him his daughter. By the way, we're boarding the plane now." The wind noise was gone.

In the background, she heard Robert Sedgwick's familiar voice. "Give me that phone."

"Senior Special Agent Yoshida, as soon as you rescue my daughter, I want you to arrest my wife. I want that bitch in handcuffs. Am I clear?"

"Yes, sir." Rayne didn't bother telling him that was already her plan. She'd allow him to feel vindicated.

Dex tapped his watch.

"Congressman, I'll take care of it."

~

With the sun halfway through the morning sky, a covert approach was going to be difficult. Thankfully, the next storm band hit and it was overcast and raining so hard no one could see anything beyond three feet. Hurricane Victor had just been upgraded to a category four and was headed straight for the Eastern Caribbean Islands. Landfall was expected on Montserrat within the next few hours, but this hurricane was so wide the thick outer bands were already whipping the Virgin Islands.

Alex's team surrounded the house perched on a very steep slope. Rayne was thrilled that Will had parked their SUV less than quarter of a mile away, hidden from view by the large house next door. The plan called for them to drive Callie down to the baseball fields. Dex and Alex would transport Angelique, under armed guard.

To everyone's surprise, there was only one exterior sentry. Remi Steele quickly interrogated the man and discovered his only form of communication with Jaja was by cell phone. The man readily confirmed that Callie and Angelique were in the house. In order to avoid more *persuasion*, he even drew a picture of where they were being held inside the house.

Rayne stood with her back against the stucco exterior, rifle in hand, her head tilted forward so the water poured off her hat. Once again, she was relegated to the second wave entering the house.. They were going in through the front door, thirty seconds behind Dex and Devon.

"On three," Dex called through their communications systems. "One."

Rayne took a deep breath and cleared her mind.

"Two."

"Holy, fuck. The door is unlocked." Ethan announced. "I repeat, the basement door is unlocked."

"Holding the count." Dex ordered, "Check all your doors and report."

Not a single door was locked. The exterior guard had admitted that he was supposed to booby-trap the doors as soon as he set up perimeter alarms.

"Changing the plan," Dex said. "We're going in quiet. On three."

"One. Two. Three." Cracking the door open two feet, Dex and Devin slid through the small opening.

Rayne started her count. At the nod from Will, she opened the door again and slid through, stepping to her left as planned. Even though all the curtains were closed, enough light came through the huge windows that she could see Devin making his way down the hall toward the bedrooms. Dex was slowly inching his way through the kitchen which opened on the far side of the living room.

Crouching down, Rayne quietly made her way through the short wide hall to the living room archway.

"Mr. Jaja, I'm sure that date is correct. My husband doesn't lie." Angelique sounded confident from her perch on the arm at the far end of the couch. "I've heard that date before, I just didn't want to tell your son the wrong information. I was going to double check it, but I couldn't figure out a way to bring it up with Robert. He's on so many important committees, you know."

If Angelique looked up, she might, possibly, be able to see Rayne. Fortunately, her concentration was on Jaja, who was sitting in the chair adjacent to the couch, with his back to Rayne.

"The only thing I know for a fact, woman, is that I'm tired of hearing you blabber." Jaja raised his gun and shot Angelique in the middle of the forehead.

Callie screamed.

Rayne's attention darted to the small ball on the couch, which she had initially thought was a pile of pillows.

Jaja jumped out of his chair and grabbed Callie. "Shut up, you worthless girl. If you don't want to end up just like her, you'd better do as you're told."

"Let go of her, Jaja," Dex ordered as he stood in the kitchen, his gun pointed at Jaja. "And drop your gun."

The terrorist instantly pulled the girl in front of him as a human shield and put his gun to her head. "No. You drop your gun."

Alex seemed to appear twelve feet from Dex, his gun also aimed at Jaja who twisted to keep them both in sight.

The man Rayne had hunted for years was less than ten feet away.

She had a clear shot.

Without hesitating, she pulled the trigger.

As though in slow motion, Aahil Mohammed Jaja's head bounced to one side before his entire body collapsed on the floor.

Callie put her hands over her ears and screamed.

Rayne sprinted into the room, grabbed Callie, and pressed the girl's face to her chest. "I've got you, sweet girl. You're safe."

Ignoring everything else around her, she started moving toward the front door.

"I'll bring the car." Will's voice filled her ear.

Rubbing her hand up and down the small-framed girl's back, she kept repeating, "I've got you. You're safe."

Dex was right beside her, reaching for Callie. "Let me carry her."

Callie screamed and tried to bury herself deeper in Rayne's arms.

As calmly as possible, she shook her head, understanding he was only trying to help. "You're a man."

He threw his arm around her and leaned in close, whispering in her ear. "A man who's concerned about *you*." He kissed her temple then stepped away. "I'll see you in St. Thomas."

CHAPTER SIXTEEN

Dex stood in the wide hallway, his back to the front door, and videoed with his cell phone the living room as Rayne would have seen it. He gave a running commentary of her movements, knowing that she was going to be questioned. It was absolutely a legitimate and necessary shooting that had been sanctioned by Homeland Security. And a damn good shot. The more evidence he could provide, the faster she could resume her normal duties.

Jaja's body still lay where he fell. So did Angelique's.

To clarify everyone's position within the room, Alex stood where he was during the shooting, and Remi was positioned where Dex had been, proving she had a clear killing field.

Turning off the movie function on his phone, Dex announced, "That's it."

"So, this is the son of a bitch who entered my island illegally and kidnapped fourteen hostages." Assistant Police Chief John Winslow carefully walked around the living room. He slid a glance at the couch. "Mart was right. That's one fucking ugly piece of furniture."

The deep chuckles of agreement eased the tension in the room.

"Dex, I want to thank you for stopping this piece of shit." John slapped Dex on the shoulder.

"I didn't shoot him. Rayne did." Dex didn't try to hide the pride in his voice. She had made one hell of a shot and without hesitation. "John, this doesn't need to be treated as a crime scene. There will be no trial. Do you have a crime scene cleanup team?"

"Yes, we have people who can handle this," John reassured. Before Dex could ask, the head of local police confirmed, "And you can trust them not to say a word. I saw the notification of news blackout."

Relieved, Dex said, "You can forward their bill to Silas Branson at Homeland Security."

"What do you want to do with the bodies?" John asked.

"I'm sure the congressman will want his wife's body returned to Virginia." Dex glanced at the woman who lay in a heap at the far side of the couch, a bullet hole in her forehead. "If you can get it bagged up and over to St. Thomas, he has a plane there. Hopefully, he can take it back with him."

"We don't have many murders here in the Virgin Islands, but I brought a few body bags left from the hurricanes last year. I'll make sure Mrs. Sedgwick is placed in one of them." John looked at Jaja's body. "What about him?"

"I wouldn't bother trying to find next of kin. Throw him out with the trash for all I care." Dex was just happy that man was finally dead.

John laughed. "Good idea. We have some heavy-duty

trash bags left from the hurricane cleanup. We'll use those for Jaja and his men."

"Sounds appropriate to me," Alex agreed. "Dex, it looks like the rain is letting up and it looks like you're finished here. Let's make a dash for St. Thomas. I really want to get my team out of here before hurricane Victor makes his appearance. I sent Jake and Zeb back to the resort to collect everything we left there. They're waiting for us at the baseball field."

"Thanks. Much appreciated." Dex turned and held out his hand to John. "I can't thank you and Mart enough for everything you did in helping us find the hostages. I hate to leave you with this mess, but we need to get out of here. Is there anything else we can do for you before we leave?"

Two of John's men lifted Angelique Sedgwick into a black plastic body bag and zipped it up.

"Take her with you." John jerked his thumb in Angelique's direction. "It could be days before we can get her off the island on a boat and we won't have any refrigeration when the electricity goes off."

Nolan and Blake appeared out of nowhere and grabbed the body bag handles.

"We've got this." Alex followed the two men out the door.

"Stay safe," Dex told John, then he walked out of the house of horrors and away from the putrid smell of death. He thought he was done with scenes like this when he retired. With one last glance at Jaja's body, satisfaction flowed through him. His personal change in status, though, didn't change the evil in the world. Terrible men like the terrorist on the floor would always be out there. So would innocents.

Dex had seen a lot of bad shit in his life, rescued dozens of hostages, but this one was going to haunt him for years. Twice he had seen Jaja hold a gun to a young girl's head. It was bad enough in the video, but standing fifteen feet away, unable to help her, seeing the terror in her eyes, smelling her fear, rocked him to his very soul.

He would be forever thankful to Rayne for taking the shot. There was gratification in watching Jaja's head explode. Then to see his magnificent woman swoop in and grab the child, protecting her from the gruesome scene. He was so fucking proud of Rayne. She was such a special and unique woman.

The mental picture he had taken of her hours before, limp from the orgasm he had just given her, naked, splayed open to him on the couch, made him smile inwardly. All-woman when she chose to be, all hard-ass when she had to be. One hell of a combination.

He wanted more of her. More of *them*. He'd left her twelve years ago, warm and sated in a bed, because his job and career had called. It happened again a few hours ago.

He was done with living for the job. Damn it, he was retired. He wanted to live for life...a life with Rayne. He could forgive her for claiming that he had hired the hookers for their men back in Nigeria. Perhaps she thought that he had. That single black mark on his record hadn't damaged his Navy career, which was now over anyway, so who gave a damn. He certainly didn't.

He wanted Rayne in his life forever. He hoped she wanted the same thing. He might just have to be persuasive enough to convince her that she wanted the same thing.

When the helicopter landed at St. Thomas airport, Dex had insisted that the other members of his breaching team fly out on the Homeland jet immediately, while they still could. He personally thanked Will Edge, Stephen Clayborn, Devin Martindale, Robert Taylor, Ethan Steadman, and Liam Bridger. He didn't need to remind them that this mission was top-secret. So far, they had been able to keep any indication of the kidnappings out of the media.

Alex and his team headed to the house they had rented. The Guardian Security pilot had given them approximately four hours to wait out the next storm band.

An hour later, Dex was determined to find Rayne. Randy Oster, the helicopter pilot, told him that she had been met by FBI agents and they were taking her and Callie to an agency facility established for the hostages.

Although Dex had never been there, the former clinic —abandoned after the duel hurricane punch the previous year—wasn't that big. It was set up like a picture frame around a lush tropical garden. As he strode down the hall, exam rooms and offices on each side, he saw Rayne as she turned the corner toward him.

"Sweetheart, I've been looking all over for you." Dex quickened his pace.

Her smile didn't reach her eyes, but it seemed as though she was trying. "I was looking for you, too." She unbuckled her holster and handed it to him, gun and all. "Deputy Director O'Brien has ordered me to surrender my weapon to you as the mission commander. After Homeland Security completes the initial investigation, and hopefully admits that it was a necessary kill, they'll turn it over to the Secret Service which will conduct its own investigation."

He reached out and grabbed the weapon and stuffed it in one of his many pockets. Then, he reached out for her. Someone exited a door at the end of the hall and turned the other direction.

He needed to touch her. Hold her. Make sure that she was okay. Glancing across the hall, he dragged her into one of the exam rooms. As soon as the door clicked behind him, Dex pulled Rayne into his embrace and held her.

"It's going to be okay," he reassured her. "We have video of the scene proving you had a clear line of fire. Jaja had been a sanctioned kill since you and I first hunted him twelve years ago. Everything will work out."

"I know," she said with confidence. "It's just, they won't let me work until I'm cleared, first by Homeland, then by my bosses, and finally, the agency psychologist has to approve my return to the field. In the meantime, effective immediately, I'm on administrative leave. I know that's standard operating procedure for any federal agent who discharges the weapon, but what if they don't clear me? What can I do in the meantime? Since mine ended up in death, it might take a month before I can go back to work."

"Even though that wasn't your first kill, you should take some—"

Rayne talked over him. "Both you and Alex may be questioned by Deputy Director O'Brien from the Secret Service because the two of you were witnesses to the shooting."

"We'll do whatever it takes to clear you." And he would. So would Alex. His gaze swept over her. "Haven't they let you shower? At least wash up?"

"They would have, but Callie refused to let go of me. I've been holding her since we left...left that house." She shrugged. "Besides, I have nothing to change into. All my clothes are over on St. John in my villa."

Dex smiled and took her hand. "Come with me. You can thank Alex. By the way, where is Callie now?"

"Still with Vanessa." She squeezed his hand. "I have to tell you; Senior Special Agent Vanessa Overholt is awesome. She was waiting for us with a team of physicians at the airport. Congressman Sedgwick was there, too, but Callie wouldn't leave my arms. She gave her dad a one-armed hug. When he looked hurt, I heard Vanessa tell him that it might be months before she trusts any man again."

Dex suddenly remembered the body bag in the chopper. "Did he ask about his wife?"

Keeping pace, she glanced up at him. "Not. One. Word. After Callie finally agreed to allow me to leave, Brian and I were able to have a short conversation, although technically, he shouldn't have been talking to me. Silas called Congressman Sedgwick just as they were landing and gave him the good news, and the bad news. All the congressman kept saying was *my daughter is safe*."

They entered a glassed-in area that had been used for patient records and reception. Their bags sat in a corner.

Bending, she grabbed her two duffels. "Remind me to thank Alex the next time I see him."

Dex grabbed his own bags and headed back out. "As mission commander, they've given me a small hotel-like room. At least it has a shower, and for now, the water is still running hot."

"You have no idea how wonderful that sounds." Her sigh shot straight to his cock.

Images of Rayne, naked in his shower, making those little mewling sounds she does when she's excited, made

Dex walk faster. "Speaking of Alex, I sent the Homeland Security plane back with the rest of the breaching team. I'm flying back in the Guardian Security plane. You need a ride?"

"No. Since technically this mission is over, my attachment to your joint task force is finished." She stopped right behind him as he unlocked the room. "Deputy Director O'Brien has asked me to fly back to DC with Congressman Sedgwick, but since I am no longer on his detail, I'm not even supposed to speak to him. I guess they don't want me talking about everything that happened."

"How soon is he leaving the island?" Dex tossed his bag on the floor.

"The pilot told us about..." She looked at her watch. "Well, we're down to three hours until this outer hurricane band passes through. We'll have a short period of clear skies to take off. How long are you going to be here?"

Dex pulled out his shaving kit. "Same." Stepping close to her, he started unbuttoning her camouflage shirt. "That means we have three hours to shower, and sleep." He kissed her then, long, slow, and very sweet. "I don't need sleep."

She shrugged out of her wet shirt, then grabbed the bottom of the tank top she wore underneath, yanking it over her head. "Sleep is overrated." She grinned up at him. "I bet I can beat you to the shower."

That was one bet he was willing to lose. Rayne did a little striptease for him as she removed each piece of clothing while he slowly unbuttoned his shirt.

Completely bare in front of him, she reached over and

stroked his erection through his wet pants. "You'd better hurry up. I might just have to start without you."

The idea of watching a woman get herself off in front of him had never been exciting before, but damn, he'd pay to see Rayne play with herself.

She was already wet and soapy when he stepped into the small shower. He used her gel to create a mountain of bubbles in his hands before cupping her breasts from behind.

"Do you still like backwards cowgirl?" He all but moaned in her ear as he rocked his erection into her tight butt cheeks while gently kneading her breasts.

"I like everything." She pressed her ass against him and moved it up and down.

He smacked her ass and she spun on him, ready to slap his face. Fortunately, he was quicker and grabbed her wrist before she made contact. "So, you don't like everything. You're not into spanking."

Her eyes flashed. "Nor am I into bondage, any kind of BDSM, and don't you ever ask me to call you *Daddy.*" She grabbed his dick and gave it a gentle squeeze. "And don't you ever try to stick this up my ass. There are only two places in my body that this can go."

She stroked his shaft and ran her thumb over the slick head. "I owe you one." She kneeled on the shower floor and took his cock into her mouth.

Dex wondered if this was a dream as he looked down at the wet black hair on the top of her head. She licked the pearl drop that had escaped before she covered his tip with her mouth, swirling her tongue. With one hand she pumped his shaft and held his balls in the other, gently rolling them. The hot water pelted his tight shoulders as the muscles in his legs constricted. She took him deeper, sucking the length, then bared teeth to the sensitive underside as she bobbed up and down.

His balls drew up tight and he knew he was close.

Grabbing her under her arms, he pulled her to her feet and kissed her, invading her sweet mouth. He couldn't remember ever tasting himself from a woman, but with Rayne, it was hot as fuck. And he wasn't going to fuck her in the shower.

He broke the kiss. "Bed." Was the only word he could choke out.

He lifted her and she wrapped her strong legs around his waist. "Hang on," he ordered.

She leaned forward and nipped at his neck. "I want you inside me." She started to lower herself, wiggling to position him at her opening.

"Condom," he said on a moan as he turned off the water and stepped out of the shower. One handedly, since the other was supporting her superior ass, he grabbed a towel from the rack and tossed it over her back. He easily carried her to the bed and laid her down on the sheets. Fumbling through his bag, he finally found the box of condoms he always carried in his go bag. He flipped a small strip on the nightstand.

Rayne laughed. "You really think we can use all of those? We're not as young as we used to be."

He grinned at her. "I still have fast recovery time." Especially with her.

"We need to be at the airport in less than three hours," she reminded him.

He bent and kissed her as he slid under the covers next to her. "Then we'd better get started."

He slid his fingers through her wet folds. Her clit was hard and swollen, begging for attention. With his thumb he circled it, pressing firmly on the top when he slid two fingers into her channel. Her walls immediately clenched in her hips bucked. She gasped in a ragged breath.

"Damn, woman, you really want this."

Rayne grabbed his face, her palms on his cheeks, and captured his gaze. "I want you."

That was all the invitation he needed. He rolled and she spread her legs wide. He quickly slid the condom over his pounding erection, having to still his entire body for just a moment to hold back his release. He was that close. But he had to make this good for her.

With his body under control, he slid the tip into her. Damn, she was tight. He couldn't remember when he had been this engorged, but she either hadn't had sex in a long time or hadn't had someone his size. "Fuck, sweetheart, you're tight."

"Please tell me that's not all you've got to give me," she warned.

He chuckled as he gave her more, giving her time to adjust. "Oh, no, sweetheart, there's a lot more."

She bent her knees and lifted her hips, forcing him deeper. "What the fuck are you waiting for?"

He bent and nuzzled her neck, kissing her just under her ear. "I love when you talk dirty."

She smacked his ass. "Fuck me, then. Hard."

He slammed into her to the hilt. "I thought you didn't like spanking."

"I don't like, or need, anyone spanking me. But if spanking you is what it takes to get this," She rocked her hips up off the bed and he swore he hit bottom. "I'm more than happy to oblige."

She squeezed his hips with her thighs and her walls tightened around his cock.

"Christ, woman, you're going to kill me. I'm so close already." He slid out and pumped back into her.

"Then get moving faster. It's not going to take much for me, either. It's been a long time for me. I think I have OBU." She met his thrust with one of her own.

"What the fuck is OBU?" He stilled and looked down at her. "That isn't some kind of new STD that I haven't heard of yet, is it?"

When she laughed, her walls vibrated around his dick, almost making him shoot off. Thankfully, the fear of a sexually transmitted disease had put it damper on everything.

"OBU, orgasm back-up," she said between laughs. It's been a long time since I was with a man, and no matter what it says on the sex toy box, it's just not the same."

He loved her little confession.

"Well, then, let's see what we can do about that." He drove into her, pulling out full-length each time.

She hadn't lied. He could feel her whole body start to tighten.

"You're close, sweetheart. What can I do to get you there?" He needed her to let go, and fast, because he was so ready. He then had a flashback to the time in Nigeria. Her breasts had been ultrasensitive.

He leaned down and took one into his mouth, sucking hard.

She exploded when he nipped her nipple.

He followed her over on the next thrust.

A moment later, he had enough sense to roll off her, pulling her in to his side. With the tissues on the nightstand, he removed the condom and tossed it in the waist can. He loved the feel of her hot rhythmic breath on his chest as they slept cuddled together.

He woke first and watched her sated face. There was something about a freshly fucked woman's face. He had given her that ecstasy and contentment. He wanted to do it again. This time, though, he wanted to show her what she meant to him. She was so much more important than a six-second orgasm.

Kissing her, he hoped to awake his sleeping beauty. She smiled and stretched, arching her back, offering him her bare breasts. Obliging, he took one in his mouth and the other in his hand, mimicking his mouth movements.

Rayne dropped her hand to his already growing erection. Her soft fingers ran circles around his dick as it hardened once again.

Within minutes, they were both ready. This time, they took it slow, savoring each other's body, building the heat within until they went off together. They held tight to each other as their bodies quaked and collapsed in sleep.

When Dex rolled over for a third round, Rayne was gone. He padded naked to the bathroom, to find her shower gel and makeup bag missing. Trotting back to the bedroom, her bags weren't there.

Where the hell had she gone? Did her plane leave early? Realizing he had no idea what time it was, he dashed past the pile of his dirty wet clothes to the nightstand where he'd left his watch.

No. Only two hours had passed.

He needed to find Rayne before she left the island.

Sweaty and sticky from hours of sex, Dex took one of the faster showers of his life. Donning clean clothes for traveling home, he set out to find Rayne once again.

"Hey, Dex, I was just coming to get you." Remi said as soon as he stepped into the hall. "The storm passed through quicker than anticipated. The pilot's ready to bug out. I'm here to take you to the airport."

Dex glanced around the quiet building. "Where is everybody?"

"If you're talking about Congressman Sedgwick and his entourage, they're already gone." Remi's word hit him like a gut punch.

Rayne was gone. She had left him sleeping in the bed they had shared. Without a word.

Fuck!

"Look, Dex, we gotta go. There's only a short break between the storm bands and we sure as hell don't want to get stuck here during a fucking hurricane. Do you need help with your gear?" Remi looked past him at the door to his room.

The room where he and Rayne had made love for hours. No. They hadn't been fucking. Maybe that first time, but after that, they were making love.

Yes. It was love. And he wasn't going to let her go.

CHAPTER SEVENTEEN

Ding, dong.

Rayne rarely had company so she couldn't imagine who was ringing her doorbell unless it was a delivery that required a signature. The Secret Service may have sent her an official letter telling her that she was on administrative leave until further notice.

Just in case, she slid open the small drawer in the table next to the front door and checked her weapon. Loaded, one in the chamber. She flicked off the safety.

She peered through the peep hole.

Shaking her head, she flipped back on the safety and stuffed the gun into her waistband at the small of her back. With the twist of her wrist the deadbolt was unlocked, and she opened the door.

"Dex, I'm surprised to see you here." She had no idea that he even knew where she lived. Reconsidering, he probably had access to unlisted addresses through Guardian Security, which spoke volumes about the company.

"Why the fuck did you leave without a word?" Dex jumped right into it.

"Because it was just sex. Remember?" She hissed. "A one-night stand to relieve stress. That's what we agreed."

"But it was more than that," he insisted.

Rayne fisted her hands and punched them to her hips. "Okay, it was oral sex, that took all of about ten minutes, and a couple of hours between the sheets. Maybe that doesn't add up to a one-nighter in your book, but it's close enough in mine."

A door banged down the street and some kids came out to play.

"We're not having this conversation on my front porch." She opened the door wide and gestured for him to come in. As soon as he stepped into the foyer, she shut and locked the door, then returned her gun to the drawer.

"Rayne, I thought we meant more to each other." He moved closer and reached for her, so she took a step back. If he touched her, she'd lose her resolve. "We worked so well together on that mission, then we had some of the best sex of my life. When I woke up, you were gone. You'd left without a word."

Good. He didn't remember her kiss. The last one she swore they'd ever have. "Usually after a quick, sex-only relationship, the two people part ways and they don't see each other again." Then she wondered out loud, "Are you upset because *I* left this time? Oh, sorry, we agreed not to discuss the past."

"Since you've already thrown it in my face, let's discuss Nigeria." Dex turned and paced into her living room. "That night meant something to me then, too. I left you in that hotel room with every intention of returning. I'm sorry, but I got called away. It was work. My whole

SEAL team was in trouble. All hell had broken loose with my men, and yours."

"I'm well aware of what happened, but that doesn't excuse you from never calling, never checking to see if I was okay." Rayne knew she had raised her voice, but she had boxed up all her emotions toward him and they had festered for over a decade. She deserved answers, especially after what she'd done for him the next day.

"I was just so angry with you," he said through clenched teeth.

"You were angry with me?" She couldn't think of a single reason why he would have been. He should have been grateful. "And I thought we had a pretty great night together."

"It wasn't what happened that night, because I agree, it was fucking incredible." He glared at her. "It was what you told the investigators the next morning."

Now she was mad. "You were mad because I told them you had spent the night with me? You were that embarrassed about admitting that you had sex with me?" She threw her hands up in the air. "Thanks!" She said sarcastically, then added, "Are you embarrassed at what happened in St. Thomas, too?"

"No." Frustration oozed from every line on his face. "I wasn't embarrassed back in Nigeria, or on St. Thomas. Fuck, Rayne, look at you." He held his hands out. "You were one fucking hot woman back then and have improved with age. I love every one of your beautiful curves. I didn't tell those investigators shit. It was none of their goddamn business who I slept with, as long as it wasn't the prostitutes."

Rayne giggled. "No. They accused me of sleeping with the prostitutes. They thought I had bought one for myself, too, because a woman in my position—what was it he called me? A ball-busting bitch—that I must prefer women over men." Her grin was sardonic. "You should've seen the look on his face when I informed him that I was strictly dickly, but even if I were lesbian, that didn't mean that I would need to pay for sex. And just because I was a female and the manager of such a large office, didn't mean that I sucked and fucked my way into that position. It meant that I was damn good at my job, evidenced by the highly successful mission the day before where we had captured six of the sought-after terrorists in Africa."

Dex burst out laughing. "Damn, I wish I'd been there to see that, especially if you had the same investigator I did."

"Balding guy with a bad comb-over?" She asked.

"Yeah, in desperate need of a shower." Dex was right about that.

"Oh my God. Yes. His body odor saturated the interrogation room and he kept leaning over me and getting in my face with his coffee breath." That was an experience she hoped never to repeat. At least her next interrogator would be Deputy Director O'Brien, or maybe even the director himself, questioning her about shooting Jaja.

She pinned Dex with her gaze. "That misogynistic prick kept hounding me about who was in my room to corroborate my alibi. It wasn't until he told me they thought you had hired the prostitutes, that I informed him that you couldn't have. You were with me the entire evening and all night."

"I didn't tell them that we were together because I was protecting you," he explained. "Those assholes were

Secret Service. Us sleeping together was fraternization. I was afraid if they found out you would be fired."

Rayne rolled her eyes. "I did almost get fired, but it was because you wouldn't corroborate my alibi. They thought I was lying. I finally had to force them to pull the hall security video that showed us going into my hotel room around ten o'clock, and you leaving close to four."

"But why did you tell them I had bought the prostitutes for my SEAL team?" He was making no sense.

"What the hell are you talking about? You *didn't* buy the prostitutes. I never said that you did." She wondered where he got that idea.

"Comb-over said that you told them that I had paid for the girls." The shock on his face proved that he believed that lie.

"Dex, investigators lie all the time," she tried to explain. "You fell for one of the oldest interrogation tricks. Besides, I knew that your chief petty officer had bought and paid for the girls to come to the hotel rooms. Prostitution is legal in Nigeria. He did nothing wrong. What the Secret Service was livid about was that my men were involved and there was video on the web, literally catching them with their pants down. Your men were there too, so that little bitch had to mention SEALs. I'm sure that metadata garnered her an extra ten thousand hits."

Dex collapsed in a side chair. "How did you find out my chief bought the women?"

Rayne walked around her coffee table and took a seat on the couch adjacent to him. "Brian, yes, the one who is my second-in-command, came and got me as soon as he learned what his girlfriend had done."

Dex rubbed his forehead. "Please don't tell me that I

have a black mark on my career record because of the jealous girlfriend."

"First, you don't have a black mark on your record. Everything about the Nigerian mission was deemed top-secret. Your official record will have pages filled with black lines where all references were redacted." Rayne took a deep breath. "I'm sorry, but this entire debacle was due to a jealous girlfriend."

"You have to be fucking kidding." Dex leaned forward with his elbows on his knees.

She shook her head. "Brian had become friendly with a freelance reporter. He thought they were just fuck-buddies. She thought they were exclusive. He had no idea that she had followed us to Lagos. When your SEAL team invited my men to share the women..."

"Yeah, I get it. They were all in their twenties coming down from an adrenaline high. The body craves sex." He gave her a knowing smile.

"We're not sure how she got into the adjoining rooms, but she caught Brian getting a blowjob. Needless to say, she wasn't happy. She slid into reporter mode and started filming what looked like an orgy. She darted out before Brian could grab her or her phone. It hit the Internet within minutes." Rayne shrugged. "You know what happened after that."

Dex reached over and took her hand. "I'm sorry. I swear, I was trying to protect you."

She interwove their fingers. "Thank you for trying to protect my virtue. The Secret Service has a morals clause, but since we didn't do anything illegal, there was nothing they could pin on me. It wasn't fraternization because I didn't hire you, nor did you work for me. We were simply two consenting adults who worked together. No one in the government was about to punish me for having an office affair, especially since I was the country's golden child for arresting the culprits who stole four million dollars using US credit cards."

Without releasing her hand, Dex moved to sit beside her. "All these years. Wasted. I was mad at you over something you didn't do. I told you I was an ass. I should've called you. It was a real dick move."

He leaned over and gave her what she thought of as the sweetest kiss possible.

Rayne dropped her head on his shoulder. "I thought you knew and just didn't want me anymore. I thought I wasn't enough for you, so you just walked away." He wasn't the first man who'd dumped her without a word, nor the last.

Dex lifted her chin so she was looking at him. "Are we good, now?"

"Yeah, we're good." And for the first time in too many years to count, Rayne was in a good place, at least in her dating life. Work was another situation altogether.

He brushed a kiss over her lips. "How are you doing? I mean, after what happened on St. John."

"I'm okay," she quipped. She couldn't lie to him. "No. I'm not okay. The flight home was weird. I'm so used to being in charge of Congressman Sedgwick's personal safety that I felt useless sitting in the back of the plane. I was little more than a hitchhiker. Brian did an awesome job. He's really good."

"I take it Callie didn't cling to you the entire trip home?" Dex rubbed his hand up and down her arm.

"No. They had given her a sedative and she curled up in her father's lap and slept. Vanessa and the FBI doctor kept an eye on her. As soon as we landed, they were all immediately taken to Quantico." Rayne forced a smile. "They'll take good care of Callie and her dad. Vanessa told me that both of them will be in counseling for years. She was more concerned with how the congressman was taking the death of Angelique."

"Were you able to sleep?" There was so much concern in his voice. No one had ever been that worried about her.

She poked him in the ribs with her elbow. "I was pretty relaxed by the time I walked on the plane. Plus, I'd had a few cat naps."

"Since you're off for a few days, tomorrow morning were going fishing." He hadn't asked, he had told her. That irked her. But she couldn't go anyway.

"I'm sorry, not tomorrow. I have to report to Homeland Security first thing in the morning to discuss the shooting. I'm not sure how long that'll take. It might be hours, or days. Then I have to go through the same thing with the Secret Service." She looked up at him and smiled. "But we'll make it fishing, someday soon." To her surprise, she was actually looking forward to it.

"What's on your agenda for the rest of today?" His hand continued slowly up and down her arm.

"Well, I've been playing domestic goddess all day, trying to keep my mind off tomorrow's inquisition." Through her west-facing front windows, she watched the sky turn a beautiful shade of orange with traces of pink. "I have finished three loads of laundry, changed the sheets on my bed, dusted and vacuumed the entire house, and I was about to start supper when you knocked on the door."

He lifted her chin and brushed his lips across hers. "Invite me to stay."

That sounded like one of the best ideas she had heard

in years. She reached up and cupped his face in both hands. "Do you like Chinese food?"

"Yeah." His voice was low and gravelly.

"Good. We'll order delivery. Later." She filled the kiss with all the need she had for this perfect man. It was voracious and insatiable. He picked her up and moved her onto his lap without breaking the kiss. When he cupped her breasts and ran his thumb over her already distended nipples, she needed more. They needed to be naked.

Hopping off his lap, she grabbed his hand and headed to her bedroom where her sheets wouldn't be clean much longer. They took their time undressing each other, learning the other's body before crawling into bed. He licked her folds and sucked her clit until she came the first time, then insisted on the second right away, using his expert fingers, stroking her hypersensitive clitoris.

When Dex reached for his jeans, Rayne stopped him.

"I'm clean. I had my annual physical about a week before going to St. Thomas. And I'm on the pill, not that there's much of a chance that I could get pregnant. I just prefer to control when I have my periods," she admitted. She waited, hoping he understood what she wanted.

"Alex made me go through a complete physical before I could join Guardian Security three months ago." He grinned down at her wet folds, then stroked a finger across them, gathering her juices before he circled her clit. "Are you inviting me to go bareback?" He clarified.

"Dex, I don't want anything between us ever again. No more lies, misconceptions, or half-truths. We're not kids anymore. We talk to each other. We communicate." Then she clarified, "and if we do this, we're exclusive." She grabbed his cock and gave it a gentle stroke. "This is mine. It goes nowhere near another woman. Am I clear?" Her heart couldn't afford a repeat of her ex-husband.

Dex slid two fingers inside her. "And this is mine. No man touches any part of your body except me." He bent down and took her breast in his mouth, swirling his tongue around her hardened nipple. When he released it, he stared at her eyes. "I've never had a problem with monogamy. You're the only woman I want."

It seemed as though he had more to say, but he claimed her lips and kissed her senseless before he slid into her, bareback. He moaned into her mouth, matching hers. The feel of skin on skin was amazing. Freeing. She bent her knees, forcing him to go deep, the way she liked it. In just a few moments, every muscle in her body tightened just before she leaped over that edge. He stiffened and groaned, then held her as they both fell, together, into ecstasy.

Waking up in Dex's arms an hour later was wonderful, but she wasn't ready for him to spend the night. Besides, she needed a good night's sleep in order to be sharp for the Homeland Security debriefing and investigation.

Neither was in the mood for Chinese, so they ordered Italian delivery and ate it at her dining room table. Rayne was pleasantly surprised when Dex helped her rinse the dishes and put away the food.

Nervously, she wiped down the counters. As she was rinsing out the dishcloth, warm hands encircled her, resting on her belly. Dex stepped into her, his chest to her back. He pulled her long hair away and kissed the back of her neck.

"Sweetheart, I would love nothing more than to carry you back into that bedroom, strip you naked, and make you come at least twice more before sinking into your heat once again."

Damn. She loved when he talked like that.

"But you have a big day tomorrow." He spun her around to face him. "I want you to promise that you'll call me as soon as you're done." He raked his fingers through her hair near her temple. "I'm concerned about you. You've been through so much in the past week." He gave her a quick kiss. "Now, walk me to the door and kiss me goodbye. I'll see you tomorrow."

At her front door, the kiss was long and slow, filled with promises.

On the front porch, he looked back over his shoulder. "Call me as soon as you're finished. I'm here for you."

"I promise." She closed the front door, flipped the locks and then leaned against it. Could the man be sweeter, and more caring?

At eleven-thirty the next morning, Rayne wanted to skip on her way out of the Homeland Security building. She quickly dialed Dex. "I'm done. Not only did they deem it a clean kill, but Silas Branson is putting a letter in my personnel jacket for my quick decision-making and excellent shooting skills. He also said that the information I provided about the people who had contact with Angelique during social events had led them to a DC-based terrorist cell. They've arrested several members and taken in over a dozen for interrogation."

"That's so exciting. Does that mean that you're free for the rest of the afternoon?" Dex sounded as happy about the conclusions as she was.

"Yes." She caught herself smiling. "You have something in mind? I could seriously use some lunch. I could hardly eat breakfast this morning, I was so nervous."

"Done. Meet me on the National Mall side of Twelfth Street and Madison Drive. I'll bring lunch."

Rayne skipped the escalator and trotted up the long stairs at the Smithsonian Station of the Metro system. As she crossed the National Mall, she noticed the hundred-year-old oak trees had started to change color. The October afternoon held a crispness in the air, but the bright sunshine held the temperature in the low seventies. Dex was waiting for her on the corner with a white deli bag in one hand and a two-drink carrier in the other.

He was the sexiest man around. Even though his eyes were hidden behind dark aviator sunglasses, she could tell he hadn't spotted her yet. It gave her a few minutes to admire the man she called hers. A full head of dark hair with silver sprinkled throughout, nearly white at his temples. He leaned against a tree, with powerful, jean-clad legs crossed at the ankles. His broad shoulders were covered in a soft denim shirt, the sleeves rolled up exposing delicious biceps.

The moment he saw her, his bright white smile flashed.

"Sunshine or shade?" He pointed to two empty benches nearby.

"Sunshine." As they walked the short distance, she giggled. "I've spent the last three days on a tropical island yet saw very little sunshine. I think that's the story of my life. One of these days, I'm just going to go to a Caribbean island and lie in the sun."

As they sat down, Dex remarked, "You said that before. Let's make that happen, soon." He opened the bag. "Ham and swiss or turkey and provolone?"

"Turkey, please."

"Name your caffeine. Coffee or Coke?" He asked, pointing to the two cups.

"I'll take the Coke, if you don't mind."

For the next half hour, they talked about her morning. Telling him about her meeting with Silas seemed so natural.

"So, now you have to face the Secret Service. Are you meeting with them tomorrow?" Dex took the last bite of his sandwich and balled up the paper.

She wasn't even half-finished with hers, but she'd had enough. She started to wrap it neatly back in the paper when Dex laid his large hand over hers.

"No. Finish eating. We have plenty of time. Neither of us has to run back to work today." He stretched out his long legs, spread his arms across the back of the bench, and tilted his head toward the sun.

He was right. For the first time in years, possibly decades, she didn't have to gulp down her lunch and rush back to work. She unwrapped the remainder of her sandwich and delved in with gusto, savoring each bite.

Answering his previous question, she said, "Deputy Director O'Brien can't meet with me tomorrow. Instead, though, he wants me to meet with the agency shrink. My appointment with him is at nine o'clock. What are you up to tomorrow?"

He dropped his hand to her shoulder and grinned. "As soon as you're done with the psychologist, we have plans."

Grinning back at him, she asked, "We do?"

"Yes. All day." He leaned in closer and whispered. "And into the night."

She had enough of her sandwich and balled the remaining portion in the paper. He plucked it from her hands and tossed it in the white deli bag. He stood and offered her his hand.

"Do we have plans for today?" She asked as she stood.

"Oh, yes. And for several hours tonight."

Hand-in-hand they walked across Madison Drive and up the steps to the Smithsonian Natural History Museum. He led her straight to the Hall of Geology, Gems, and Minerals where they stood in a short line so she could see the Hope Diamond.

They caught dinner in a little bistro a few blocks away, then took the train back to the Department of Homeland Security where she'd left her car.

"Hop in. Where's your car? We can go get it, then if you'd like to—" she was about to suggest they go to her place for a nightcap, and a little more.

"Not tonight, sweetheart." He kissed her with all the affection she wanted his hands, his lips, his body, to show her.

A black BMW SUV with darkened windows pulled into the lot and headed straight for them. Rayne automatically reached for her weapon. Before she could pull it out, Dex stopped her with a hand to her forearm.

"That's my ride, sweetheart." He gave her a quick kiss. "I'll see you tomorrow." He held open her door and waited until she turned out of the parking lot before jumping into the big black vehicle. That's when she saw the Guardian Security logo on the side.

As she drove to her home in Virginia, thankful that traffic was relatively light, she played her day over in her mind.

Best. Day. Ever.

CHAPTER EIGHTEEN

Dex wasn't sure if he should congratulate himself or kick his own ass. As he crawled into the bed at the Guardian Security apartment, he knew he could be sliding between the sheets at Rayne's home.

Except he didn't want her to get the idea that he only wanted her for sex. No. He wanted her forever, and he was willing to take it slow.

Even though he wasn't on an assignment for Guardian, Alex said he could stay in their office building in downtown DC anytime he wanted. The invitation had come just after Dex had sold his house in Virginia near Little Creek, so he was between homes.

The company had an entire floor of apartments, plus a penthouse for when Alex or his partners were in town. It seemed they had the same set-up in every one of the ten offices. He had stayed in a similar apartment while overseeing the mission in Venezuela. The rooms were furnished closer to an upscale condo than a one-bedroom studio. He had everything he needed, except a private place to bring Rayne.

Knowing he would see her tomorrow, thoughts of her filled his mind as he fell asleep.

Dex smiled the next morning around ten-thirty as he checked his caller ID and saw that it was Rayne. "Good morning, sweetheart. How did it go?"

She sighed. "He wants me to go to Angelique's funeral...tomorrow...in West Virginia. He thinks I need closure on that fucking bitch."

Dex didn't withhold his laugh. "I'm sorry, but I have to agree with the shrink on this one. Watching her body go into the ground may be therapeutic. What time shall we leave?"

There was silence.

"We?"

"You didn't think I was going to let you go there alone, did you?" He thought about it for just a moment. That would be minimum eight hours driving if they went up and back the same day. Since he was sitting at his computer, he typed out a quick email to Alex asking if he could use the company jet, and explaining why.

"Why would you want to go with me?" She was obviously walking through the parking lot toward her car.

"Because I want to be there, for you. What are you wearing?"

"Clothes," she clicked back.

"Okay, let me rephrase. Are you wearing comfortable clothes and shoes that you can walk in for at least five hours?" He had another adventure in mind.

"Yes to the comfortable shoes, but no to the comfortable clothes." She explained, "Mother nature decided today should be winter, but like an idiot, nervous about talking to the psychologist, I walked out of the house without a warm coat. If I were going to spend time outside, I'd also put on a turtleneck sweater."

"Go home and change into warm clothes. I'll be there in an hour to pick you up." Before she could argue, he said, "You'll love what I have in mind for us today. See you soon."

Two hours later, they watched the Giant Panda Bears easily climb a tree. The fall chill had kept the tourists away, so they didn't have to fight the crowds at the National Zoo. They strolled for hours, reading every sign, discussing some of the animals they had seen in the wild. Rayne smiled almost the entire time.

They strolled down the block to an Irish pub that had been recommended to him by one of the men working at Guardian. He hadn't steered them wrong. The food was authentic, the beer cold and the atmosphere realistic.

This time, when Rayne had invited him to her place for a nightcap, he took her up on it.

"You serious about riding with me to West Virginia tomorrow?" She asked as she sat up in bed, the sheet falling to her waist, exposing her naked breasts.

"No. Because we're not driving. We're flying in the Guardian jet." He moved his pillow against the headboard and sat up next to her. "The funeral is at two o'clock. We'll grab some lunch, then go to the private airport. The pilot told me he'll land at Greenbrier Valley Airport, a small landing strip about eight miles from the church, which is next to the cemetery." He leaned over and kissed her, fondling a breast. "We'll be home before supper." He bent down and took one breast in his mouth, rolling her other nipple between his thumb and forefinger. He knew that turned up her heat from sizzle to burn.

As they slid back under the covers together, he asked, "May I stay the night?"

She stroked his already stiff cock, then straddled him, sliding him into her. He'd never get tired of sex with this woman.

"You try to leave, and I'll hold you here at gunpoint." She moved up, squeezing her butt cheeks, tightening her inner walls.

He never wanted to leave.

They touched down at one o'clock the following afternoon. A car and driver were waiting for them and took them straight to the church.

As they stood in the vestibule, Vanessa greeted them.

"I'm surprised to see you here," Rayne blurted out.

"Callie and her father are still living at Quantico. She doesn't want to go home, and to be honest, I don't think she's ready. We have a child psychologist who sees her, and a few of the other girls, every day. Ms. Rogers tutors her in the afternoons after her own therapy session. Lynda and Charlotte Thompson and Elianna Martin will probably be with us for a while as well. The psychologist thought this would be good for her, but he didn't want her here without support."

"Sounds like my shrink," Rayne interjected.

Vanessa smiled. "It *will* be good for you. It may take you a week, a month, or a year, but believe it or not, watching them put her in the ground will help you emotionally deal with her death."

Dex could feel her tension mounting, so he placed his hand on Rayne's back and moved it up and down. Her breathing eased out.

Rayne stared at the small gathering of people in the church. "Are those her parents?"

Vanessa scoffed. "You mean her *dead* parents? That woman was a piece of work. She'd fucked up that little girl's mind so bad. I can only hope the psychiatrist helps Callie work through all the lies that she told her. It's going to take years to build up that child's self-esteem once more. And the way the bitch kept her from her father...."

Vanessa shook her head. "He's in just as bad a shape. Feeling guilty for marrying Angelique, guilty for allowing her to take over their lives, the late-term abortion is truly beating him up, then there's the whole Jaja thing. He's considering not running for reelection again and concentrating on his relationship with Callie."

The minister walked to the pulpit and looked around.

"I think we should take a seat." Dex put his hand at the small of her back and guided Rayne to a pew in the back of the church.

Dex hated funerals. Although he was glad to see this terrible woman buried, it brought back so many memories of good men—his men—that he had to lay to rest. His thoughts of war, too many missions to count, the thousands of hours of training, the faces of the SEALs he had commanded throughout his career, filled his mind.

Rayne nudged him with her elbow, bringing him back to the small church in West Virginia and the funeral of a terrible woman. He still couldn't decide whether Angelique was the best actress he'd ever met—or the most stupid, unlucky woman. Perhaps a bit of both.

They were the last ones out of the church and stood far away from the family. At the end of the service, as they turned to leave, Callie sprinted toward them, followed closely by a woman dressed in a black pantsuit, crisp white blouse, reflective aviator sunglasses and an earbud.

At the obvious recognition, her Secret Service protection slowed and approached quietly.

The little girl threw her arms around Rayne. "Thank you for killing Mr. Jaja. I hated that man."

Dex noticed several people with wide eyes at the child's loud declaration.

"And thank you for saving me." Callie shook in Rayne's arms. "I thought he was going to shoot me, like he did Angelique."

He watched as Vanessa nodded to Rayne. His woman wrapped her loving arms around the young girl. Tears streaked down both their faces. "I know." Rayne's voice was tight and cracked. "I wasn't going to let him hurt you."

"I love you, Miss Rayne." Callie buried her face in Rayne's shoulder.

"I love you, too." Rayne dropped her face, hiding it from everyone.

Dex watched Congressman Sedgwick approach. "Senior Special Agent Yoshida, thank you for everything you've done, including this." He gestured to his daughter. "She hasn't cried since you left her in St. Thomas."

Vanessa stepped forward and put a hand on the Congressman's arm. "Callie has to do this on her own. I believe she'll move forward now that she's seen Rayne here."

Callie lifted her head and sniffed. "When will you be coming back to us?"

Rayne shrugged and rolled her lips in, making her mouth a straight line. Dex knew she was trying to hold in all her emotions. "I don't know. I'm not even sure they'll allow me to supervise your detail anymore."

Callie whipped around and ran to her father,

throwing her arms around him. "Daddy, tell them that Miss Rayne has to come back. We need her."

He kissed his daughter on the top of the head. "I'll see what I can do." He looked at Vanessa at his side and asked, "I think we're ready to leave. Can you get Callie back to the car for me, please? I'd like a word with Senior Special Agent Yoshida."

Vanessa held out her arm. "Come on Callie, let's get out of here." They left with an arm around each other.

"You've been with us for so many years, and through so much, standing stoically at our side, I hope you don't mind if I call you Rayne."

"Yes, sir. That will be fine." She squared her shoulders and held his gaze.

"I read the reports," he held up his hands. "Yes. I know they're top-secret, but I think you'll understand my need to know what happened. That terrorist deserved to die just for taking my child." He tilted his head back to the grave. "And she deserved to fucking die for putting my little girl in the hands of that fucker." The Congressman's voice shook with anger. "Because of that fucking bitch, thirteen innocent lives have changed forever." Then he corrected himself. "I guess I need to expand that number to include the parents and siblings of all those girls." He shook his head. "I'll never be able to make it up to them. Never." He choked out the last word and pulled his sunglasses over his eyes.

Holding out his hand, he said, "And I'll never be able to thank you enough for bringing my little girl back to me —in more ways than you'll ever understand."

Rayne took his hand in hers, then stepped into the man she had protected the last three years. She hugged him and sniffed back a tear.

Stepping apart, she added, "Take care of her. She's such a precious and strong girl. She's going to be a magnificent woman someday."

They turned and walked off in different directions toward the cars.

Rayne intertwined her fingers with Dex's. "Thank you for coming with me. I'm not sure I would've made it through this without you."

"I'll always be here for you." He hoped she understood the magnitude of those words. He had no intention of ever letting her go again.

On the flight home, she was quiet for so long that Dex began to worry. "What's on your mind, sweetheart?"

"The future." Her words rocked him.

Dex knew what he wanted for their future—the two of them, together. Forever. Just as he was about to tell her how he felt, she started talking.

She turned partially in the seat toward him. "I'm not sure if I can go back to protecting Congressman Sedgwick."

That was not at all what Dex had expected her to say. He was ready to blurt out personal futures and she was talking career. Okay, he could flow this direction. He had counseled several younger officers when they had considered leaving the Navy. Hell, he'd been through it himself when he'd reached twenty years.

"Let's talk it out," he suggested.

"You saw us at the funeral." She threw her hands up helplessly. "We've moved beyond Secret Service agent and protectee. I have been his bodyguard for three years and he has never once called me Rayne. That alone moved me into a more personal category in his mind, and to tell you the truth, mine."

"Okay, so you can't be in charge of Congressman Sedgwick's safety, but surely you're capable of protecting someone else." Dex wanted to be sure she realized her value.

"There are only two other positions higher than mine in the field." She continued to explain, "the next step up would be coordinating the detail for the Vice President. After that, there's only the President."

"Are you telling me that you wouldn't want to be in charge of the Presidential security detail?"

"Yeah. I think that's what I'm saying." Her eyes looked desperate for acceptance. "I know both the men who run those details. They're both divorced. They eat, sleep, and breathe their Secret Service job. I already can't remember the last time I took a day off besides this forced leave."

"I can tell you when you're going to take the next day off, and what you're going to do." He said smugly. "You owe me a day of fishing. Since that's going to take place on Smith Mountain Lake, you might need to take off three full days in a row."

"I'm not going to know what to do with myself," she professed.

He leaned over and gave her a light kiss. "I'm sure we can think of a few things. What other jobs can you take within the Secret Service?" He understood that she needed to work her way through this.

"I don't really want a desk job." She grinned. "Besides, if you're sitting behind a desk, they don't like it when you shoot somebody."

He grabbed his tablet and opened the website for federal jobs in the DC area. There were thousands. "Looks like you have a lot to choose from."

She slipped the tablet over and entered a different website, one exclusively for currently employed government workers. She searched by her current employment rating. Five jobs popped up.

"No. No. Fuck no. No fucking way would I do that job for what I make now. And, last but not least, there is no way in hell they can hire me."

Dex had to agree with each of her analysis.

"I have to confess, I'm getting too old for this job. I had a hard time keeping up with the rest of the team. I'm embarrassed what a difference ten years can make."

Dex laughed out loud. "I'm going to let you in on a little secret. The last three years when I commanded a SEAL Team, it was nice not to have to keep up with those new recruits. These old knees couldn't run as fast, jump as high, or take the beating that they could at twenty-four. Except for enduring through pure tenacity, I doubt I could pass BUD/s again."

"If I had stayed in the Navy, I would've retired this year. I would be moving on to something else anyway." She sipped some of her water. "On the flipside, if I hang in there with the Secret Service for seven more years, I could retire with a nice, constant income. I'd be close to my fiftieth birthday, and still have plenty of energy to go out and have fun, at least for a few years, in retired life. Plus, I could break a few more glass ceilings, making it easier for younger women to reach the higher ranks in the Secret Service."

"That's a very valid point," Dex agreed. "Now playing devil's advocate, that means you will continue to work sixty or more hours a week, and rarely take a day off to go fishing with me." He wondered aloud, "You talk to your girlfriends about this kind of thing much?"

She scoffed. "What girlfriends? I don't have time for friends. The only people I'd even place in that category are the men that I work with because they occasionally invite me to go out and have a beer with them. Oh, and they invite me to their weddings. I think I told you, divorce is high among Secret Service agents. So are the number of weddings. At least they keep trying to find a good relationship."

That admission gripped Dex's heart. He decided to put a positive spin on her depressing statistics. "And see what happens when you quit looking? A good relationship finds you." He punctuated his statement with a kiss to show her how much she meant to him.

As they sat back in their seats, he discovered his water bottle was empty. "I think I need a drink. I'm pretty sure there's some wine, beer, and some damn good scotch back there. What's your poison?"

"I'd love a glass of white wine. I can come back with you and get it. Besides, I want to check out this airplane." She glanced at her watch. "I've never been tempted before to join the mile-high club, but I've never been alone in a luxury jet before either."

"Your wish is my command." He demonstrated how the seats could fully recline.

An hour later, the captain announced they were landing and should finish any drinks. He reminded them that all glassware needed to be placed in the dirty dish rack.

"A very nice white wine," Rayne noted as she handed the empty glass to Dex. Grinning, with that satisfied-woman look on her face, she asked, "What do I get for joining the mile-high club?"

Dex placed the crystal glasses in the secure rack. "You

already got it. In your case, an orgasm at forty-two thousand feet, several miles above the earth."

She looked around the cabin as they made their way back to their seats. "Do you travel like this all the time? Congressman Sedgwick does, but I'd expect him to have this kind of luxurious lifestyle."

He chuckled. "In the Navy, we rode in the back of cold, stinking helicopters that were almost as old as I am. With Guardian, though, we always fly private. We usually carry too much weaponry to be allowed on a commercial plane."

She sat down and buckled in. "I could get used to this lifestyle."

As he sat beside her, he suddenly remembered Alex's invitation. "We've been invited to a party tonight, at Alex's fiancée's condo down on DuPont circle. You were just telling me you don't get out enough. I'm sure you can meet some interesting people there. Want to go?"

"Absolutely. Gives me a chance to thank Alex for this plane and remembering to grab my clothes from the villa. Maybe I could get to know him better."

Dex was so pleased with her response. He couldn't wait to show off the woman in his life.

CHAPTER NINETEEN

Rayne had to admit; she was a bit nervous as Dex drove into the parking lot of the DuPont circle condominium. But she was there for him. Reciprocating, because he'd been there for her at the funeral. She truly appreciated him listening as she hashed out her future. Everything was still up in the air, though. She still had to go through the Secret Service investigation. Then there was the agency psychologist. He should be happy that she attended Angelique's funeral. Wasn't sure what closure she got out of it, but it was wonderful to see Callie was doing well.

Dex came around the car and opened her door. Such a gentleman. He also held the door to the lobby open for her so she could enter first. As they stepped to the elevator, she examined her outfit one last time. She chose to go a bit more feminine tonight. She wore a pair of tailored slacks with a gold silk blouse she had bought on a whim because it felt so soft against her skin and was on sale for less than half price. She topped off the outfit with a black sweater trimmed in gold. Her black flats had tiny gold trim as well. Her ankle holster was also black, not that anyone should see it.

Damn, Dex looked good. He wore a light blue button-down dress shirt under a navy blue sweater and dark blue dress pants. It looked as though he had shined the ever-present black boots. Maybe they were a dressier version of the ones he always seemed to wear.

Dex had to insert some kind of card, then pressed the button for the top floor.

"This apartment belongs to Alex's girlfriend?" She asked nervously.

"Fiancée," he corrected. "I think they"ve been engaged for quite a while, though."

"Most of the other people here will be people you work with?" She had no idea why she was feeling anxious. She'd met several of the men, and truly liked Alex.

Dex ran his hand up and down her spine and her anxiety seemed to dissipate. "It's just a party. If you start feeling uncomfortable, we'll leave."

The door opened on the top floor and the party seemed to be everywhere. It looked as though there were only three units, one on the left and two on the right.

"Dex. Rayne." Alex greeted her with an unexpected hug. He shook Dex's hand and then pulled him in for the backslapping, one-armed man hug. "Food is in each apartment. Kat's been cooking all day."

"Oh, dear. I could've brought something." Rayne felt sorry for the poor woman who spent the entire day in the kitchen. She was probably exhausted.

Alex laughed. "Cooking is Katlin's way of decompressing. They just got back yesterday from a six-week mission in the Middle East. We have these parties when they return mostly to consume all the food she cooks."

"And, so we can catch up on our wine consumption," the pretty redhead with gorgeous green eyes said as she walked by arm-in-arm with the tall man with broad shoulders.

"Griffin," Dex called, and the man turned with a huge smile.

"Dex. How's the fishing?"

He pulled her closer to him. "Parker 'Griffin' Mitchell the Third, I'd like you to meet my..." He looked at her as he hesitated. "Girlfriend seems such an inaccurate name because, sweetheart, you are all woman."

Rayne didn't know whether to blush or smack him. She chose to ignore Dex and held out her hand. "Rayne Yoshida."

"Nice to meet you, Rayne. I'd like you both to meet my fiancée, Grace Hall." Turning to the redhead, he continued, "Grace, this is Dex Carson. He spent a few months in Miami with me while coordinating the Venezuela mission."

Dex leaned in close to Rayne's ear. "Griffin is the manager of Guardian Security's Miami Center." He then looked at Grace. "Did I hear that you're a Navy Lieutenant? A pilot?"

Griffin and Grace exchanged a look before she said, "You are correct. I'm a Navy Lieutenant, and I am a pilot. Our team is attached to Homeland Security, though."

Curious, Rayne asked, "Are other members of your team here?"

Grace dropped her head onto Griffin's shoulder. "We're all here. Celebrating because we finally finished that mission." She leaned up and gave Griffin a kiss.

"Six weeks is a long time to be away from the man you love."

"Come meet the rest of the team." She picked up her wine glass and licked the last drop from the rim. "I need another glass of wine. You need one, too. Griffin, Dex needs a drink."

Grace hooked her arm in Rayne's and led her into the apartment on the left. Within minutes she met Dr. Nita Callahan and her husband, Daniel, and saw beautiful pictures of their little boy and baby girl. Next came Tori, who could be a runway model and owned one of the condos down the hall. She was in a relationship with Marcus, an ATF agent. Lei Lu, a petite fireball with delicate features, was sitting on the lap of a man named Zane.

Last, but not least, Rayne finally met her hostess, Katlin Callahan. After a few moments' confusion, she finally sorted out that Daniel was her brother.

"You're the one who killed Aahil Mohammed Jaja." Katlin smiled and held up her hand for a high five. Their smack seemed loud in the packed kitchen.

"Finally. It only took me twelve years, but that's one terrorist who will never kidnap another young girl." Rayne filled her plate with food that looked too pretty to eat.

Katlin gave her a perceptive grin. "I know exactly what you mean. My team has a very unique mission. I hear you're a Secret Service agent. Tell me about that."

Rayne found herself twenty minutes later talking to Katlin as though they had been best friends for years. She'd even confessed that she may be looking for a career change. It must've been all the wine.

"Let me get this clear. You like being in personal

protection, you just don't want to do it twenty-four-seven, three hundred sixty-five days a year." Katlin had narrowed the problem down to one sentence. "You might also be interested in traveling some, is that correct?"

"Yes. I'd love to be able to pass the reins off to someone else after eight, ten, or twelve hours, and maybe even get a few hours of free time." Might as well shoot for the stars, Rayne thought.

"Okay, come with me. We need to find Alex." Katlin started with her place, but didn't find her fiancé there, so they headed down the hall. At the last apartment on the opposite side of the hall, Katlin strode in through the open door.

Alex and Dex sat in chairs talking with a man next to a very pregnant woman on the couch.

Katlin turned to Rayne. "Have you met Harper and Rafe Silva? This is their place. Silva family, meet Rayne Yoshida."

"I'd get up and shake your hand, but I'm being forced to sit here with my feet up," Harper complained.

"She's retaining water and it's not good for the baby," Rafe explained.

Katlin walked over and sat on Alex's lap. "You're the managing partner but I think Rayne would be a perfect addition to our DC office in the personal protection division."

Both Dex and Alex looked at Rayne.

"You're leaving the Secret Service?" Alex asked.

At the shocked look on Dex's face, Rayne thought she ought to slow down the Katlin steamroller. "I'm considering it as an option. I haven't been reinstated, yet, and although Homeland Security has cleared the shooting, my agency hasn't finished their investigation."

Alex's gaze darted between Dex, Katlin, and Rayne. He stood with Katlin in his arms, as though she weighed nothing. Then he placed her in the chair he just vacated. "Come on, Rayne, let's talk. You might be just the woman I've been looking for to fill a very unique vacancy in our DC center."

Rayne was glad she was sitting down when Alex talked salary and benefits. It was a perfect job.

"Take a few days. Think about it. Give the Secret Service time to do their investigation, then you can make an informed decision." Alex stood. "I think I'm going to go find Katlin and see if she's ready to go home."

Confused, Rayne asked, "Isn't this her condo?" She looked around the magnificent five-bedroom apartment. It took up the entire side of the building with a wall of windows looking toward the National Mall.

"Yes. This is her place, but we usually stay in our penthouse at Guardian Security."

"It's nice you call it *our* penthouse." Rayne thought that was so sweet. "But I guess you'll be married soon, and it will belong to both of you."

Alex chuckled. "It's always been our penthouse. I may be the managing partner of Guardian Security, but she's my silent partner...who's not always so silent."

Suddenly Rayne felt terribly guilty. "Are you hiring me because Katlin told you to?"

"I think I told you before, that we have a woman in personal protection out of our New York City Center. When you come to work for us, I'll send you to work with her for a week or two. She and Blake often take jobs together so they can travel around the world."

"Thank you, Alex. I'd appreciate it if you could give me a few weeks. I'd like to clear things up with the

Secret Service first." In her alcohol-hazed brain, she refused to think about that inquisition. Out of nowhere, she added, "I think I might take a vacation before I go back to work."

"Rayne, you take as much time as you need." Alex looked out the door of the study where they had been talking privately. "Right now, I need my fiancé."

She followed him out of the room. "I'm going to go hunt down Dex."

On the way home she told him about the offer. "What do you think?"

"Sounds pretty damn good to me." He reached over and took her hand. "I really like the idea of us working together. I'd love to see the world with you. But how about tomorrow, we tackle the Air and Space Museum?"

"I like that plan," she admitted.

That night, when she crawled into bed next to Dex, he simply pulled her against his naked body. "Go to sleep, sweetheart. You've had a big day."

She curled into his warm body, falling deeper in love with him. Somehow, he knew that she needed to be held that night. Although she would have had sex with him, had he pressed, but he didn't. He was such a wonderful man.

He had been twelve years ago, too. He had tried to protect her honor. What a sweet, and thoughtful man. Rayne listed every man she had dated in the past twelve years and realized she had measured each one against Dex. None could even come close.

She wondered if she was in love with him back in Nigeria, but the adult in her now understood that they couldn't have made it back then. They were both young and too career-focused.

Listening to his slow, even breathing, she wondered if they could make it now. Was he worth taking a chance?

Fuck. Yes.

Rayne let out a deep, contented sigh. She was falling in love again, with the man who she'd fallen in love with twelve years ago.

Over the next week, Deputy Director O'Brien rescheduled their appointment three times. As directed, Rayne made daily visits to the agency psychologist. She was becoming more frustrated that they couldn't conclude the investigation and clear the shooting. When she expressed this to the psychologist, he claimed it was the natural progression, just another stage she had to work through before she could be reinstated.

Alex's offer sounded better every day.

Dex was there for her, day and night. After every appointment with the psychologist, they would grab lunch, then stroll through another Smithsonian Museum.

In late November, as they exited the National Gallery of Art, the freezing wind threatening sleet by the time they reached home. Rayne suggested, "I think we need to leap forward to that tropical island on my bucket list."

Dex gave her that smile that she considered just for her as he pulled his knit hat over his ears. "So, when did you figure it out?"

"When you showed me the Hope Diamond," she admitted, then trotted across Madison Drive onto the National Mall. She pulled Dex off the path, allowing one of the huge oak trees to shield them from the wind. She pulled off her gloves so she could touch him. Placing her palms on his already chilled cheeks, forcing his complete attention on her, she confessed, "I love that you listened. I love that you are checking things off my bucket list. I love the way you make love to me. I love that sometimes you just hold me at night. Dex, I love *you*."

She pulled his face to hers and crashed her lips on his. It was as though every emotion ever pent up within her body exploded in that moment. She couldn't get enough of him and didn't want to ever fill that void completely. She would always want Dex Carson.

Panting, their moist breath freezing into clouds, they stood wrapped in each other's arms, foreheads touching.

"I don't have pretty words like you do, but you have to know, Rayne, that I love you. I want to spend the rest of my life with you." Dex glanced away then recaptured her gaze. "I hadn't planned any of this, so if I fuck it up, I'm sorry." He rubbed his thumb over her cheek. "Rayne Yoshida, will you marry me? We can go right now to any jewelry store you want to pick out a ring. We can do it together, like we can do everything else together for the rest of our lives."

Rayne was in shock. She had hoped that Dex loved her, but there had always been the possibility that he wasn't ready to say those words, or share those feelings. She had never in a million years expected him to say that he loved her in one breath and ask her to marry him in the next. She hadn't thought ahead to marriage.

"Rayne, sweetheart, I need an answer before we freeze to death in this nor'easter." He shook his head. "I told you I was going to fuck it up. Take all the time you need. I'll be here. Well, I'd rather not be right *here* because this is going to be one hell of a storm." He pulled her away from the tree and they started down the block toward the car. "Come on, it's going to take us twice as long to get home in this weather."

As they passed the Museum of Natural History,

Rayne glanced toward the bench that she now thought of as theirs. She didn't need to think about it. Spending the rest of her life with this wonderful man was exactly what she wanted. She stopped and pulled him around to face her. "Yes. I'll marry you."

"I love you, and always will." His kiss was filled with promise, and only ended when she started to shiver. "Can we honeymoon in the Caribbean? Soon? Like next week?"

THANK YOU FOR READING THE SILVER SEALS SERIES BY THE SUSPENSE SISTERS

SEAL Strong - Cat Johnson
https://www.silverseals.com/books/seal-strong-silver-seals-series-prequel/
SEAL Love's Legacy - Sharon Hamilton
https://www.silverseals.com/books/seal-loves-legacy-silver-seals-book-1/
SEAL Together - Maryann Jordan
https://www.silverseals.com/books/seal-together-silver-seals-book-2/
SEAL of Fortune - Becky McGraw
https://www.silverseals.com/books/seal-of-fortune-silver-seals-book-3/
SEAL in Charge - Donna Michaels
https://www.silverseals.com/books/seal-in-charge-silver-seals-book-4/
SEAL in a Storm - KaLyn Cooper

https://www.silverseals.com/books/seal-in-a-storm-silver-seals-book-5/

SEAL Forever - Kris Michaels

https://www.silverseals.com/books/seal-forever-silver-seals-book-6/

SEAL Out of Water - Abbie Zanders

https://www.silverseals.com/books/seal-out-of-water-silver-seals-book-7/

Sign, SEAL and Deliver - Geri Foster

https://www.silverseals.com/books/sign-seal-and-deliver-silver-seals-book-8/

SEAL Hard - J.M. Madden

https://www.silverseals.com/books/seal-hard-silver-seals-book-9/

SEAL Undercover - Desiree Holt

https://www.silverseals.com/books/seal-undercover-silver-seals-book-10/

SEAL for Hire - Trish Loye

https://www.silverseals.com/books/seal-for-hire-silver-seals-book-11/

SEAL at Sunrise - Caitlyn O'Leary

https://www.silverseals.com/books/seal-at-sunrise-silver-seals-book-12/

ALSO BY KALYN COOPER

Black Swan Series

Unconventional Beginnings: Prequel (Black Swan Novella # 0.5)

Unrelenting Love: **Lady Hawk (Katlin) & Alex** (Black Swan Book #1)

Noel's Puppy Power: **Bailey & Tanner** (A Sweet Christmas Black Swan Novella #1.5)

Uncaged Love: **Harper & Rafe** (Black Swan Book #2)

Unexpected Love: **Lady Eagle (Grace) & Griffin** (Black Swan Book #3)

Challenging Love: **Katlin & Alex** (A Black Swan Novella #3.5)

Unguarded Love: **Lady Harrier (Nita) & Daniel** (Black Swan Book #4)

Choosing Love: **Grace & Griffin** (A Black Swan Novella #4.5)

Guardian Elite Series

Double Jeopardy (Novella #2 Guardian Elite series crossover with Hildie McQueen's Indulgences series)

Justice for Gwen (Novella #2 Guardian Elite series crossover with Susan Stoker's Special Forces World)

Rescuing Melina (Novella #3 Guardian Elite series crossover with Susan Stoker's Special Forces World)

Snow SEAL (Novella #4 Guardian Elite series crossover with Elle James Brotherhood Protectors World)

Securing Willow (Novella #5 Guardian Elite series crossover with Susan Stoker's Special Forces World)

Cancun Series

Christmas in Cancun (Cancun Series Book #1)

Conquered in Cancun (Cancun Series Novella #1.5)

Captivated in Cancun (Cancun Series Book #2)

Claimed by a SEAL (Cancun Series Novella #2.5)

Never Forgotten Trilogy

A Love Never Forgotten

A Promise Never Forgotten

ABOUT THE AUTHOR

USA Today Bestselling author KaLyn Cooper writes romantic suspense based in fact. Twenty seven years as a military wife has shown her the world and the men and women who protect it every day. Thirty years in PR taught her fact can be stranger than fiction, but she leaves it up to the reader to separate truth from imagination. She and her husband live in Tennessee on their micro-plantation filled with gardens, cattle, quail, and a bird dog. When she's not writing, she's at the shooting range or paddling on the river.

Contact KaLyn

For all the latest info, check out **KaLyn's website**
www.KaLynCooper.com

Sign up for exclusive promotions and special offers only available in **KaLyn's newsletter** http://www.
kalyncooper.com/newsletter.html
Email: KaLyn@KaLynCooper.com

 facebook.com/kalyn.cooper.52

twitter.com/KaLynCooperbooks

instagram.com/kalyncooper

bookbub.com/authors/kalyn-cooper